Blood-tie

Austere and unhurried, aloof in his spats, grey gabardine and tall, celluloid collar, Sir Bertram Pendleton, eminent pathologist, infallible expert in murder, boasts a thousand post-mortems a year. When he appears in court, looking like the great undertaker-in-chief, lawyers defer to him as if he possesses some queer, authoritative, almost supernatural understanding of death.

Contentedly overworked, moving around the country from case to case and always seeming to spend afternoons in slow trains, arriving at dusk in empty station hotels, Sir Bertram finds in a cadaver a sanctuary, certainty and beauty by contrast with which the world outside is bleak.

But there is another side to the man the papers call 'a legend in his lifetime'. Dreams of subversion have resulted in a dark, secret life in which Teddy, Roddy Rockinghorse and a ballet tutu play essential roles, a private domain of which only his beloved sister Ivy is the guardian. Poor dear big-boned Ivy, with her Player's No 3, her defective hearing aid, and her tentative, doomed interest in men.

In this bizarre and entirely absorbing story, Stephen Coulter dissects, with great subtlety, wit, and delight in the macabre, a sinister sibling relationship, and reveals the dangerously deceptive sanity of a pathological mind.

By the same author

Threshold (1964)
An account to render (1970)
The château (1974)
The Soyuz affair (1977)

BLOOD-TIE

Stephen Coulter

Constable London

First published in Great Britain 1988
by Constable and Company Limited
10 Orange Street London WC2H 7EG
Copyright © Stephen Coulter 1988
Set in Linotron Palatino 10pt by
Redwood Burn Limited
Printed in Great Britain by
Redwood Burn Limited
Trowbridge, Wiltshire

British Library CIP data
Coulter, Stephen *1914–*
Blood-tie
I. Title
823'.914[F]

ISBN 0 09 468630 0

To Nadine
with love

1

Occasionally, on these journeys, an English fellow-traveller entering the second-class compartment and, instantly calibrating the symbols of caste, would betray a twinge of recognition and for a moment sit searching for the deciding clue to the middle-aged figure in the corner seat, suety ewe face under the grey Homburg hat (banking or the Ministry of Pensions? upper third of lower half of upper middle class?), the spats, grey gabardine, the phenomenally tall celluloid collar and loops of gold watch-chain, a faint touch of the Victorian, austere, grave and unhurried. A few might inconclusively note the black bag in the rack above. But on this raw January afternoon nobody had got in and Sir Bertram Pendleton sat alone as the train trundled across the northern English countryside, the well-adjusted heating making his head muzzy and the draught freezing his shins.

This was twenty months before he wore the tutu to dinner in London for the last time.

Rain squiggled on the glass, blurring the sooty landscape beyond like fog through which, as they rounded a bend, the train in silence seeming to slow progressively with floating dreamlike leisureliness (as if the driver, seeing something indistinct and still invisible to the passengers had not yet made up his mind to stop) loomed the sodden, motionless group, still clogged as it approached then resolving itself into two policemen and four detectives in bowler hats, all peering down behind the canvas screens sagging in the wet and wind, into the waterlogged trench, no, grave, now close up, where he believed he saw, then actually recognized, himself in the process of stamping to free his cold feet from the mud beside the coffin whose lid . . .

Sir Bertram jerked his head upright, shook himself, his mouth dry; that had been the last case. Shifting and stamping his feet, he probed with forefinger for the gold half-hunter in his waistcoat pocket, flipped it, a dim dab of butter, into his palm. Five minutes past five; ten minutes more.

Folded on the seat beside him nestled the early edition of the London morning paper, his picture on the front page under the headline *Sir Bertram in the Box*. The picture showed him arriving at the court, pitched forward as he walked, tall, lean and 'distinguished', carrying the same black bag . . . the figure of authority, the man they called 'a legend in his lifetime'. In the white space at the bottom of the page was:

STOP PRESS
Maharajah Divorce Case
(see this page)
Mrs Barnes told court she met Maharajah
at reception for HRH Prince of Wales.
Welstead Murder Verdict
Giles found guilty, sentenced to death.

Naturally, it had been inevitable.

The respectful breathing lapped round the courtroom, against the witness box where Sir Bertram Pendleton stood upright, jaunty, irrefutable, undeniable, his black coat with fresh rose buttonhole and professional striped trousers, his celluloid collar and collar-stud signifying cool command. The eyes and necks filling the court repeated the respectfulness of the breathing. Old Mr Justice Dearest's pen sputtered.

Carstick KC, for the Defence, weaved and jerked his head like a boxer taking a punch each time Sir Bertram said, 'No, that is quite impossible,' or 'No, there was no trace.'

'But Sir Bertram, we have heard eminent medical authorities here say that there were distinct marks.'

'I found no trace at all.'

'Is it possible – I ask with all respect, Sir Bertram – is it possible that you missed them?'

8

A rustle like windswept tram-tickets from the listening courtroom.

'I missed nothing.'

Interposed old Dearest: 'I think, Mr Carstick, we may leave it at that.'

'As Your Lordship pleases.'

The public benches cooed approval. He could already see the late edition placards: *Sir Bertram demolishes Defence*. And Dearest saying, in his summing-up, 'All who heard it must have admired the clarity and force of Sir Bertram's evidence. Sir Bertram could find no room for doubt as to the cause of death. And I would remind the jury that there is no greater authority on these matters than Sir Bertram Pendleton.'

He had not waited for the verdict. In a month's time he would perform the post-mortem on Giles, another contribution to his research on judicial hanging.

A ghostly signal-box sailed past followed by a huddle of pale walruses or cows nosing the fence. He pulled his gloves on, foreseeing, apart from the cadaver, what lay ahead at Ditchley – the miserable hotel (no return train until tomorrow), the awful food which he swallowed as a kind of unnecessary yet somehow compulsory penance, self-imposed along with these constant train journeys, the overwork, the routine, the mean two-guinea fees, a second-rate asceticism. A moustache appeared under a veined nose; the Chief Constable now was . . . Hurd? Bird? Two or three years since his last visit? . . . three, the abortion case. His lips compressed, his face lengthened and behind the long gleaming mahogany table the bald heads, black coats and professional striped trousers of the British Medical Association struck off the head of the culprit he had stalked and laid before it; whereupon the ex-doctor, head in place but wobbly, was lounging back obscenely in white flannels waving a glass of deadly absinthe on a white stone terrace on the Côte Something – Côte d'Azure, refuge of murderers, abortionists, artists, foreigners and other unsavouries.

The last lumpy fields went by under the low sky. The train was slowing down. On the platform, four burly bowler hats approached, shiny with wet, as if they had lost him a few

9

minutes earlier at the dream-like exhumation and had just trudged in.

'Colonel Bullah, Chief Constable,' said the brush moustache. 'Glad to see you, Sir Bertram.'

Mouth tight, he nodded dryly as Buller introduced the detectives and the local doctor, all of whom eyed him obliquely.

'We have the coroner's order.'

No fuss; they knew he wouldn't have it. They marched – Pendleton gave a skip to put himself in step – towards the station entrance where for some reason they had posted a fat helmeted police constable who, as they appeared, began to twinkle on ballet points in the direction of the waiting cars.

'Eh . . . ?' Buller, hunched forward, marching beside him, turned his head, looked up inquiringly. Pendleton's face was expressionless. 'Er . . . where was I? Yes, a disused factory, place is a ruin, hasn't been used for years but she must have been there quite some time. Unpleasant sight – but . . . well, h'm . . . daresay you're used to that, Sir Bertram?'

Sir Bertram Pendleton made no answer and Buller coughed. 'Far as we know . . .'

Bottling plants went by, identical streets of depressing slate-roofed houses, lace-curtained, dark and unheated, red-brick chimneys, demonic cinema posters ('This Week *Thou Shalt Not*. Coming Attractions *Dawn* with Sybil Thorndike and *With Cobham Round the Cape*'), the sudden mystic flowering of the name Magnicor Road (a Victorian battlefield?) until, after the last public house, they arrived at a wrecked building standing on its own, backed up against the raw fields. Dusk was falling; everything looked gloomier and more depressing. The car doors slammed. He followed the bowler hats picking their way among the bright pools of water across the mud of the yard, and stepped cautiously in among the detritus of paint drums, glass, rusting iron, bricks, faeces, collapsed roof girders until, in the middle, they were looking down into an oblong vehicle-repair pit half-filled with rubble and pools of water with bluish oily streaks.

'There,' Buller said. 'We've searched the place but . . .'

Sir Bertram Pendleton nodded; they seemed to be waiting for an observation, a question; he said nothing. They drove back in silence into the town. The corner building where they alighted presented a Boys' Brigade notice (Buller in a stupid pillbox hat tilted sideways held on by a black lacquer chinband, one of a moustachioed Victorian regiment in the Zulu wars) – the Boys' Brigade hall was evidently used when necessary as the coroner's court, since Buller led the way behind it to a grey cement-floored hut, the coroner's mortuary, and stood back for him to enter. The hut had not recently been washed out. A sixty-watt bulb swung under the porcelain reflector, the drain was choked. A brown rubber sheet covered the threatening mound on the slab. Unhurriedly Pendleton took off his coat and hat, hung them up, changed into his long white apron and gloves, arranged his bottles, tubes, sponges, instruments and specimen jars on the damp green wooden bench and lifted the sheet off. Silence . . . some gritty feet-shifting.

The cadaver, a woman's, was greenish, partly decomposed, features bloated, left arm half extended, palm open, both knees half bent, lower lip swollen to a sausage, the unconcerned expression of death, yellowy adipocere forming on one cheek and both breasts, thick dark curly hair, characteristic crescents of rat bites along the legs. It had been surgically opened down the middle, four ribs had been removed and the shiny inner contents dumped roughly back in a pile.

Sir Bertram Pendleton stood studying the body, bent over, nose close to the skin. Behind him a match flared. Immobile, Sir Bertram Pendleton said tonelessly, 'No smoking. I have to smell.' It was his private joke; his sense of smell had gone years ago. A bowler hat went outside.

'. . . an accident,' Thwaite, the police surgeon, was saying. 'No obvious cause of death, at least from what I could see, though of course if . . . She was in a curious position, doubled up, possibly, it occurred to me, because she'd tried to move, found she couldn't and . . . I had to straighten her out to do the PM.'

'As I say,' Buller said thickly through his red snuff handkerchief, 'as I say, the place is sometimes used by courting couples, believe it or not. Our first conclusion was that she'd – well, the doctor's told you that. But the coroner . . .'

'Photographs of the position she was found in?' Pendleton said.

Mumbles from the handkerchief. 'I . . . er . . . not *in situ*, no. We have those when she was brought here, of course.'

'Pity. Great pity.'

Above the handkerchief, Buller's eyes watched the hand in the pale skin-tight glove insert itself into the whitish heavy-looking apron-like mess, a finger delicately lift a flap, uncovering a recess of deeper reddish moisture with pipes and tubes. Pendleton peered inside, the finger probed here and there, lifted. Buller hummed a few bars of 'Tea for Two' to himself and when he looked up again Sir Bertram Pendleton was walking slowly round the body studying it. He opened the right hand, examined the palm. The right leg held his attention; he bent closely over one area on the thigh about six inches above the knee, then over an oval-shaped mark a little higher.

'Birth-mark or an old bruise,' said Thwaite.

Pendleton passed wordlessly on, examining the calf, turning his head at various angles, eyes close to the skin. At the head, he ran his hand lightly through the hair, passed it this way and that, abruptly peered at one spot high up on the right side, parted the hair and exposed a small hole in the skull.

'Ah.' Thwaite's neck extended, he gave a short laugh. 'Confess I didn't notice that.'

'She shot then?' Buller thickly burbled.

'This is not a bullet wound, 'Pendleton said. 'Help me to turn her over, doctor.' The same close inspection of the head and body lying in the prone position, they turned it back again, pushing the organs back into the peritoneal cavity. With a tape-measure from his bag, Sir Bertram Pendleton measured the cadaver, muttered the result to himself to memorize it.

'One thing I haven't mentioned, Sir Bertram . . . I mean, she was dressed, of course. She was – we've got the clothes, the blouse was the wrong way round, label in front, you understand? The label . . . Unless she took it off for somebody.'

'H'm . . .' Sir Bertram Pendleton was quickly snipping away the hair, handed the hanks to Thwaite. 'Mind shaving the head, doctor? Careful here, I'll do this part.' He produced razor and cream from the bag, handed them to Thwaite. When this was done, Sir Bertram Pendleton made one cut across the top of the head from ear-top to ear-top with the scalpel and another from the base of the nose across the top of the head to the back. Then, reaching for a chisel, he applied it at an angle to the cut on the crown of the head, gave it a knock with the heel of his hand and proceeded to peel away two flaps of scalp, one after the other, pulling each well down over the face.

The detective uttered a throaty sound. Buller gazed intently at his shoes which grew a double edge, refocused. When Pendleton had in turn pulled the two rear flaps of scalp down over the neck, he laid the chisel between the breasts, picked up the scalpel again and, making another cut, this time round the head in the temporal region, inserted the handle of the scalpel between the muscle and bone, lifted off each temporal muscle and pushed it down. Carefully he scraped the muscle attachments off the bone. Etching the scalpel across the exposed skull bone, he cleaned it thoroughly, paused and rummaged in his bag, and extracted a thick rubber band. This he slipped round the circumference of the skull, adjusted it until it was about an inch above the eyebrows and, using it as a guide, drew a blue carpenter's pencil line round the skull.

'Hand me my saw, Dr Thwaite . . . and while I am sawing, kindly turn the body as I direct. Keep the mallet and chisel handy just there, please.'

'I . . . ah . . . Mind if I step outside, Sir Bertram? I have a telephone call . . .'

Forty minutes later, Sir Bertram Pendleton snapped his black bag shut, put on his coat and hat. Buller and the detectives came back into the shed. They did not look at the slab.

'She was murdered. Age between thirty and fifty. Time of death three weeks ago, maybe four. The murderer killed her by driving a spike or a nail six or seven inches long into her brain, probably while she was asleep or unconscious. Dr Thwaite's finding her blouse put on back to front indicates that she was undressed. I can't tell if she was drugged until I have my samples analysed. She was killed somewhere else and taken to that factory site. The doubled-up position of the body indicates that she was hidden somewhere first, probably in a wooden crate. The upper part of the body was wrapped in sacking at some stage; you can see the pattern of the sacking. There are also faint marks of the side of the crate on her legs and I have a splinter from her leg when she was forced into it. The murderer found he could not get her completely into the crate, her right foot protruded, he had to force down the lid and when he did this he broke a bone in her foot.

'I have taken skin samples with the crate marks on them, also the area with the mark which Dr Thwaite thought was a birthmark. It looks to me like tar. I shall know positively when I have analysed it. The exact chemical composition may help us.'

'You'll be making your report to the coroner in the usual way, Sir Bertram?'

'Naturally.'

The bowler hats edged forward. 'Can you give us any clue, Sir Bertram?'

'Look for a firm in the area that uses seven-inch spikes or nails in its business, perhaps to fasten heavy crates for transport. Heavy engineering crates possibly. I found three tiny pieces of metal in her buttocks, possibly metal shavings she picked up from the floor of the crate. The spike could have been a bolt that had been sharpened on a metal lathe. Somebody who had access to crates and a metal lathe – and sacking – whose wife or friend disappeared in December. I will let you know the wood the crate was made from.'

'Well, I think we all deserve a noggin after that little lot, eh?' one of the detectives said.

'We've put you up at the Railway,' Buller said. 'And Mrs Buller and I hope you'll give us the pleasure of dining with us tonight. We're particularly proud of our – '

'Thank you, but I shall be writing up my notes and my report,' Sir Bertram said.

'Ah yes, of course.' Buller hadn't really expected Sir Bertram Pendleton to accept but he was nevertheless simultaneously relieved and put out. By all accounts, Sir Bertram was not very approachable, not a mixer, and from what they said, dull, no talker. Just as well. 'Well, if you'll allow me to drive you over?'

When he came down to dinner after writing up his record-card, the report on the autopsy and filling in the official forms, the dining-room was empty except for two couples at different tables, conspiratorial over four domes of bright yellow pudding. The waitress, handing him the bill of fare, confided that the fish was very nice tonight and Sir Bertram Pendleton, after briefly considering the alternatives, resignedly nodded, sat back. Anything to drink? Sir Bertram's upraised palm forbade the thought.

The orange wallpaper of the room was decorated with a tasteful design of multi-coloured parrots alternating with old crocks. A massive sideboard displayed a row of mustard-pots and a glass bell under which two sandwich-lips were beginning to snarl, showing pale pink tongues. The decorous silence was disturbed only by the sussuration of the couples, the passage of the waitress, the occasional slap of a door beyond; and, as he often did in court, Sir Bertram tingled with desire for an act of subversion. Dressed as a Samurai, he stalked in, squirted a bottle of warm beer over the others and, sitting down, calmly set fire to the tablecloth. Elbows on the table, hands on either side of his face, fingertips touching his cheeks, he was aware of the woman of the farther couple eyeing him. It would really need nothing violent, merely simple incongruity . . . the repeated puffing of one cheek?

The blankness of the evening stretching before him, the probability of waking in the middle of the night (he could already hear the shriek of a train-whistle signalling rain) had, as usual, banished his fatigue. Again as usual, he had the old nagging anxiety at the back of his mind about Ivy, dear sister, at home, though this was so shot through with loving tenderness that it was somehow numbed. Of course this room, the lighting of his bedroom above, the hopeless ugliness, still present, of those houses they had passed this afternoon, the projected existence of the young man over there, keen to succeed as Assistant Marketing Manager of some piddling firm, any of these could, in a moment, depress him, make him irrationally afraid. Outside the domain of his virtuosity, the world was bleak, by contrast with which the cadaver this afternoon, the deformed mouth, the face as he sawed off the top of the skull, offered sanctuary, certainty, beauty, a code he understood, the familiar probes, the old familiar sections, discolorations, burnings, inflammations, petechial haemorrhages, tissue reactions and so forth, where he was king (rivals often declined to appear against him if they knew he was going to appear for the other side), a reason for pride, and intense aesthetic pleasures, visual and tactile – nothing, at all events, to be afraid of or depressed about. But was it only because it had occupied him for so many years, that the idea of anything else was unsettling? A question to which he had no answer.

'What's that – no answer?' Old Dearest cocked an eye. 'We must all agree with Sir Bertram that there is an answer to everything. And no place for half-truths. Not in a British court of justice – that has fortunately been recognized long ago.'

Waiting solemnly for his dinner, Sir Bertram Pendleton shifted his knife and fork. Before him, on the tablecloth, interlocking grey lines on the white surface outlined a polyptych where the cloth had been ironed or misfolded or impressed by rectangles, or drawn on or damaged in manufacture. The folds or panels made a lidless bottomless box standing on the cloth, the front panel folded outward for half its breadth, then becoming a full panel. But abruptly, as Sir Bertram looked at it, this was the side panel of a different box sideways on and below the first . . . Wait a minute, try again. The third side of the lower box was the inner panel of the first box or the fifth fold of a box (or folding fire-screen) seen from below and thus floating above the cloth . . . Sir Bertram glanced away, looked back. The four and a half folds of the upright form refused to yield to the second form, if there was one, of which they had seemed, a moment ago, to be part. But when he tried now to keep the form in place while he followed the lines to completion, the folds switched places and the second form persisted. He shifted his eyes . . .

Fortunately, the waitress appeared, bringing his fish. Sir Bertram contemplated the plate, raised his head to ask what it was, but the waitress, interpreting his instant of hesitation as acceptance, had turned away. Never mind. He picked up knife and fork . . . Make a median incision next to the vertebral spines and reflect the subcutaneous tissue laterally . . . cut the posterior layer of the thoracolumbar fascia about two millimetres from the median plane, beginning above the level of the iliac crest and extending superiorly. Continue the cut transversely, reflect the flap laterally to the lateral edge of the erector spinae muscle where it joins the middle layer. Make a longitudinal cut through the middle layer so as to expose the posterior aspect of the quadratus lumborum . . .

Placing his diary on the lateral edge between the median plate and the table-edge, he finished his dinner looking over the appointments awaiting his return; tomorrow the analysis with Walker, before anything else, at the hospital; 11 a.m. Wednesday, Judson, at Director of Public Prosecutions (Page case); telephone Bowen, NW Paddington coroner 3 pm. Thursday (Todd case); Taggart KC, 4.30 in chambers; Friday afternoon Kent County police (Madcap Cottage case; don't forget fresh samples). Arnold asking him the other day why didn't he get a secretary to type up his notes, make his reports? Because he preferred to do things himself.

The waitress approached again; the blancmange tonight was really lovely. Sir Bertram Pendleton declined. No dessert at all? No thank you. He gave his room number, pushed back his chair and stood up.

No telephone in the room, naturally; but there was a glass-panelled booth next to the reception desk with a lopsided notice 'Please Give Room Number', on which somebody had scrawled a male member. He asked the operator for a trunk call. Eventually Ivy's pale voice answered. She had finished supper half an hour ago, was listening to the Home Service, they had just been playing Dvořák's 'New World' Symphony (mentally he registered a thumbs-down; poor Ivy's musical taste was nowhere, she loved Albert Ketelby and Coleridge Taylor). Was he all right? . . . No, no messages. Oh yes, Dr Walker had rung up to ask if would be back tomorrow; she had said she expected him; then that was all right. Nothing else, no. Well, then, all was well. He kept her on the line, transmitting reassurance to her, seeing her as the young girl with her fair hair down her back, a ridiculously out-dated but dearly treasured image – she was now somewhat faded and thirty-seven. Then he rang off.

The black rectangle beyond the front door gleamed with

rain; cars hissed by. A ballooning raincoat trudged by led by a sodden chow. The manager, a man with a cocklike crest of red hair, was inclined to be chatty, but Sir Bertram, who never talked for the sake of mere talk, asked for an early call, with tea, and went upstairs. The green linoleum on the floor was chilly. Having washed in cold water at the washstand and disposed of the slops, he unlocked his suitcase and took out his teddy bear. With teddy on the pillow next to him, he composed himself for sleep, knowing that he would wake in a couple of hours.

2

The oval mirror (from Mother's mother) hung on two simili-bronze chains with gold tassels above the mantelshelf, over the mahogany-cased clock which had just let out a distinguished cathedral-like chime for twelve-thirty. Ivy, having dusted the mantelshelf, took care to replace the two green china doggies in the correct diagonals at each end, then on either side of the clock, respecting the angle, the two framed photographs, one of Mother and Father in the garden (Father, already looking puffy, gazing off to one side, six months before his death; Mother still two years away from her last illness), the other of Boudie and herself, arm in arm, in the same spot. And finally, in spite of the asymmetry, the small snap of Girlie, their beloved Airedale, her look so human you would say all she lacked was a speaking voice.

Twelve-thirty! She had lost track of the time again this morning. Boudie would soon be here and she had not yet prepared lunch. She bent down and, lifting the brush from the fireside brush-tongs-poker set, quickly flicked it over the pale-lavender tile surround and the pinkish-brown logs in the fireplace, straightened the hammered-metal kerb and stood back. There. Curious how a fireplace denoted people's status, particularly the surround and the sort of fire (theirs was electric, of course, splendidly modern, in which, when it was switched on, the logs glowed most realistically).

She paused to survey the room; it was rather too crowded with furniture – but how fortunate they had been to keep all Mother's and Father's things; the rod-backed narrow-seated benchlike seat with round cushions, so smart and pre-war

19

(Father and Mother had been resolutely 'modern' as anyone could see from the four arched niches in the wall beside the fireplace, each containing a china faun in different dance poses), the glass-fronted china cabinet gloriously crowned by the figure of the old woman balloon-seller holding her bunch of different-coloured balloons, Ivy's favourite from childhood, the large oval picture, untitled, which Father always explained was allegorical, of a woman in a crinoline waiting in the shade of a tree with five black and white dogs – a valuable work; and, pendant to this, the picture of the colonnaded front of a building (the Cotton Exchange, she thought).

Beyond the lace curtains of 41 De Vere Gardens, the morning light was an unbroken flat grey. The sound of a step beyond attracted her attention, but next moment she realized it was not her brother but Mrs Tickner, her next-door neighbour, who had come in the back way. She turned, thumbing the amplifying dial of her hearing aid, an expression of doubt on her mild plump face. She had never used make-up, her pale eyebrows failed to dramatize her blue eyes, her fair hair, which today she wore in a large bun at the back of her head, was neither curly nor lustrous. She might have made up for this rather seal-like, erased look by her mouth; her upper lip was provocatively short (photographs of her when young showed a delicious cherub-like pout); but something about her front teeth, a shade too large, and the shape of the lower lip destroyed any babyish appeal. Her body was large and well-made.

She moved to the door, shut it behind her, determined to receive Mrs Tickner in the kitchen. Ivy did not really like Mrs Tickner; for one thing, though she was over fifty she hennaed her hair, not a very bright red but a biscuity gingerish shade. She smoked little Woodbine cigarettes (much inferior to Ivy's own Player's No 3) and knocked the ash off them by simply bumping her hand against furniture. And then Mrs Tickner was . . . well . . . curious; always asking questions about Ivy, about Boudie, and their doings.

Of course, as Mother had explained, it was jealousy. The two families, the Pendletons and the Tickners, had always lived next door to each other in these two houses – Mrs Tickner

20

was the only surviving member of hers – but for some really strange reason, the Tickners had had the idea that the Pendletons were 'queer'. Oh, this wasn't just imagination, oh dear, no. Ivy knew it for a positive fact, she had heard it years ago from Mother who had had it confirmed by old Mrs Ashpole. Mrs Tickner had naturally never as much as hinted anything of the sort to her or to Boudie. But jealousy it was, nonetheless.

The Tickners, who had never been professional people (they had inherited the house or they would never have lived in the district) had always aspired to the Pendletons' social standing and it was still necessary to make the distinction between them clear. When Boudie's knighthood had come through (Ivy had learned it was smart to speak of it as 'a K'), Mrs Tickner hadn't called on them for three solid days and then had gushed so much you would have thought she had personally recommended it to His Majesty. Nobody, of course, would be deceived but it was an oblique attempt to put them on the same footing.

'My dear, I can't find my keys again – did I leave them here?' Mrs Tickner said briskly. 'Don't disturb yourself.' Mrs Tickner repeatedly used this as an excuse to 'pop in' unexpectedly and poke around. She was small and bright-eyed. 'I see they've called Sir Bertram in on that, what do they call it, the Ditchley Mystery Death.'

'Yes, he's coming back this morning.'

'Oh? What did he tell you about it?' Mrs Tickner always faced her and spoke in an extra-loud voice with exaggerated lip movements. Ivy turned down her hearing aid which was crackling with the extra volume.'He never tells me, you know.'

'He must tell you something, my dear. I mean when you talk in the evening. I'm sure he lets you into the secrets.'

As usual, Ivy felt on the defensive. Mrs Tickner's eyes were taking an inventory of the kitchen, which she already knew by heart – large round table overhung by green-shaded Liberty lamp, wooden chairs, the bijou scullery with yellow pleated curtains, a replica in design of her own kitchen but better furnished. 'I see that poisoner Giles has decided not to appeal.'

'I'm not surprised,' said Ivy. 'Bertram was so definite. He

couldn't be shaken.'

'That's the phrase they always use, isn't it?' Mrs Tickner said somewhat sarcastically.

'It was a triumph for him over all those other medical men, don't you think? The way he dealt with that ridiculous Dr Redpath.'

Mrs Tickner twitched her lips censoriously but said nothing.

'All the papers reported the judge's praise for him, you saw that?' Ivy said.

'My dear, I was saying to myself this morning that if I asked you nicely, you'd show me that satin-wood dressing-table my mother always admired so much. You mentioned it yesterday, which reminded me. Do you think you could?'

'Oh . . . I don't know . . . ' Ivy was beginning to feel nervous. Mrs Tickner was always trying to see the upstairs rooms, inventing one pretext or another. And as she gazed at her, Mrs Tickner became a long-beaked bird with a red cap and a ruff of feathers circling her neck. 'Only take a minute,' Mrs Bird Tickner said. 'Just a peep.'

Her round red eye fixed Ivy, her claw lifted, scaly and spiked. Mrs Tickner flew up over her head, perched on her hair. Fortunately at that moment the key sounded in the front door lock and Mrs Tickner rapidly came down, excused herself and left. Sir Bertram Pendleton deposited his suitcase, hung up hat and coat and entered from the hall. Ivy patted her hair back into place.

'Hello, Boudie, dear. I hope you're not too tired.'

He kissed her cheek, arm around her shoulders, gazed smilingly at her. 'Are you all right, my darling?'

Dr Percy Redpath steered majestically out between the columns of St Edward's Hospital with young Dr Wilfred Carr in tow as Sir Bertram Pendleton, back from Ditchley, walked up the entrance steps carrying suitcase and black bag. They passed in silence. On the pavement below, Carr said, 'Wasn't that Pendleton?'

'Was it?'

'Pretended not to see us.'

'Well . . . ' Dr Redpath, a large, naturally expansive man, yellow wavy hair poking out from under his black Homburg hat, carried himself in full sail. 'Did you see what he said in court the other day? "I have applied my mind to the question of . . ." I have applied my mind! I ask you!' They laughed together. 'At the end, the judge said to the jury, "You have listened to Sir Bertram Pendleton. You will ask yourselves if you ever heard a witness who more thoroughly impressed you with his fairness, his absolute impartiality, who more completely satisfied you with his demeanour, the clarity of his evidence."'

'Who was that, Dearest?'

'No. I think it was Chatfield . . . yes, Chatfield. But they're all the same. They all love him. He puts things so simply. It's all black or white. He doesn't live with variables. He's always got a definite answer. I don't know how many propositions there are in medicine you can answer with a flat yes or no – but he never has any difficulty. And he's absolutely certain – Oh, taxi! . . . Damn it.'

They walked on. 'The thing is', Redpath said, 'he's understood the way lawyers' minds work. He loves it when they split the question up into little bits that he can answer yes or no to. You know the ploy – or rather, you don't yet but you will – "We are getting into technical matters here, doctor. I think it will help the jury if we can take this step by step." Doesn't matter if it distorts the thing – the old boys on the bench won't see that. They love his certainty. Never a doubt! They treat him as an expert in murder; that's what he is, an expert in murder. He's infallible. Merely by being on a case he makes them feel that everything depends on the autopsy – that that's the key – that's where the answer lies.'

'I hear they've asked you to appear for the Defence in the Rooksby case?'

'Yes. If I can get a decent look at the body. They've applied for an exhumation. And this is precisely – precisely – where Pendleton has an advantage: he sees everything first, he's very thick with the police, that's his job, he's practically an honorary member of the CID. And if you put up against him you probably see the cadaver after it's been buried a couple of months and he says, "Oh, I saw such and such. You can't see it now? Sorry." I've even seen it happen with his samples: "Well, it *was* there"! And what can you do? H'm? If you don't agree, he just says you're wrong, and they'd much rather take his word for it than yours. He sees the prisoners' statements to the police before any other medical man. As a medical witness he's allowed to sit in court from the start of the case, magistrate's court and so forth, hears all the evidence, so the Prosecution can call him again: "Sir Bertram, you have heard what Mr So and So says. Is that consistent with what you found?" All he has to say is "No," and it's done with. They take his word for it. The situation's preposterous.'

'I asked Ormond about him, says he's not much of a mixer.'

'Solitary bird. Bit . . . er . . . I dunno . . . bit *queer*. Contradict him and he gets huffy. Case goes against him – which is very rare – he won't talk to the other doctors. Keeps himself to himself. Never see him in the middle of a lunch party or in a pub. Has lunch by himself, takes a book or a paper so that nobody interrupts him.'

'Hates cricket, they say.'

'Oh, you couldn't drag him to a Test Match. He couldn't even tell you who Bradman is.'

'You're not serious?' Carr's voice expressed shock.

'Taxi . . .!'

In the pale green and brown pathology laboratory on the first floor of St Edward's, Sir Bertram buttoned his white coat, lifted the jars of samples one by one from his bag and arranged them in a row on the bench with the cards he had written up the night before; the formalin, rubber gloves and instruments he placed to one side.

Walker, the analyst, was bent forward peering at the jars, each sealed and labelled in Sir Bertram's spiky hand. 'These are Ditchley, then?'

'H'm?' Sir Bertram sounded somewhat abstracted. 'What was that fellow doing here, do you know?'

Walker straightened up somewhat baffled, hovering, but quickly connected; 'that fellow' meant Redpath. 'Was he here

– this morning? I didn't know.'

'Leaving as I came in. Didn't come up here, I hope?'

'No. Not as far as I know.'

In a flash Sir Bertram saw the Palace grounds, the royal garden party, Queen Mary radiant in silver-grey and turquoise, looking seven feet tall, challenging a cringing Redpath to show his invitation card for which, of course, he fumbled in various pockets in vain – whereupon she whacked him over the head with her cream parasol and two liveried footmen, balancing silver trays, frog-marched him out across the lawn to tremendous cheers from the other guests. He swallow-dived back to Walker, rubbed his hands together; the laboratory was never warm.

'Well, now – Miss Noakes. What have you got there, the liver?'

'Small. 1.150 grammes,' Walker said, consulting his notes.

'I noticed the kidneys were small too.'

'Eighty-nine grammes each. Some congestion, as you see.'

'All right. Now what did you find?'

The tap dripped into the sink.

The telephone rang just after the Home Service nine o'clock news. The forecast was 'Very unsettled' with a gale warning; rain was falling. Ivy laid down the *Tatler* she had just opened and Sir Bertram answered. It was the CID, Detective Chief Inspector Skinner.

'Sorry to disturb you, Sir Bertram, but . . . ah . . . fact is, I'd very much like to have your assistance . . . yes, tonight . . . I'm sorry. A case that's just come up. It'll mean driving down to Sussex, the coast . . . no picnic on a night like this, I know, but . . . Well, we've detained a man, I'd like to leave it till the morning but I don't think we should waste time. As I say, I hesitate to – '

'That's perfectly all right, Detective Chief Inspector. How long will you be?'

'About half an hour.'

'I'll be waiting for you.'

Ivy touched her hearing aid, gazing anxiously from the

25

other side of the fire. 'Do you really have to go tonight, Boudie?'

'Yes, my dear. Something in Sussex. Don't know how long it'll take but I'll let you know as soon as I find out. You'll be all right, h'm?'

'Take a scarf and your heavy raincoat.'

When the black police Humber saloon drew up outside, it waited with motor ticking. Nobody got out. At No 43, a curtain moved. Sir Bertram slammed the front door of No 41 behind him, carrying his bag, crossed unhurriedly to the kerb with his collar up and climbed in beside the bulky man in the back. 'Evening, Detective Chief Inspector.' A flash of him eating a newspaper with tea in front of a propped-up kipper.

'Good of you to turn out, Sir Bertram. You know Detective Sergeant Nichols, I believe?' The man beside the driver twisted round and Sir Bertram nodded.

'Where are we going?' Sir Bertram said.

'Place called The Shingles, near Lynford. Let's get on, Ramsay. Trees down in this, I shouldn't wonder.'

Sir Bertram Pendleton drew on his tight-fitting gloves. He admired the idea of tight-fittingness, compression. For this reason he sat upright; it was necessary outwardly to assert order, cohesion, the principle of regularity. Thereafter subversion was more enjoyable. The dark draughty interior of the car smelled vaguely of wet mackintosh and police boots; complex skeins of light streamed past, shoals of light-fish, the tyres hissed, the two decapitated heads – the driver and the bowler-and-ears of Sergeant Nichols – wobbled against the faintly glowing windscreen in front. The Sergeant's ears were remarkably prominent. They would vibrate audibly if twanged.

'I'd better tell you about the case,' Skinner said. 'The man's name's Kelso, the man we're holding, Arthur Kelso – we haven't charged him yet, all we've said is we're detaining him "for further inquiries" – that's why I've asked you to come along tonight, Sir Bertram. He's the, you know, bouncy, talkative type, several convictions, one six years ago for molesting a woman he'd diddled out of some money. Did four years. Married a respectable girl when he got out. Far as we know he's been working . . . far as we know. A friend, about a fortnight ago, a friend of the wife's, that is, told her she'd noticed him at Waterloo station with a woman. This made her, made the wife, think a bit, especially about Kelso's absences, supposed to be "on business", and she started to keep an eye on him. Eventually, we don't know how, she found out that he'd left a bag with a friend of his at Fulham, friend working in a Fulham garage. She thought this might give her a clue to who the woman was, the paramour was. So she told a cousin of hers, that is, the wife did, a cousin who'd been in the auxiliary police; he collected the bag and got it open. It gave him a surprise – there was bloodstained clothing inside, including a pair of bloomers, a bottle of disinfectant, Jeyes' Fluid, and a butcher's saw. He brought it to us.

'So when Kelso called for the bag Thursday, we were there. He tried to make a joke of it, laugh it off, first of all, said he'd been slaughtering a pig down in the country. We took him in but, as I say, we haven't been able to charge him yet. All he says is he wants to "consider his position". After one of my men found the return half of a ticket to Lynford in his raincoat pocket, he admitted he'd rented a house there but says he hasn't been there lately. For the moment that's all we've got to go on.'

'Thin.'

'Very.'

They drove on in silence. From time to time, Sergeant Nichols gave the driver a direction. At the coast, the rain came bucketing in bringing the smell of seaweed, cockles-and-vinegar. The car rocked. They passed the sheds of the seaplane base, patches of windy open ground with scraggy undergrowth, a wagon or two of shingle ballast on the rusty branch track of the London, Brighton and South Coast Railway. A half-demolished sign said *Bovril for* – In the gloom, in the gloom of his soul, the fronts of the high-class boarding establishments, Private and Residential, went by: Every Modern Comfort; Gas Fires in all Front Rooms; Terms Strictly Moderate; Refined and Homelike; Resident Proprietress. Ahead, at the end of the straggle of cottages and bungalows, they saw moving lights and figures. These turned out to be a group of police officers from the East Sussex Constabulary hunching in

27

the wind and rain with hurricane lamps and flashlights. Brief greetings and introductions between blue noses and chilled fingers, and they all trooped over the uneven ground to the house.

The others stood back, Sir Bertram and Skinner entered the uninviting room, no doubt called 'the lounge' – drunken chintz-covered settee, two upright chairs, yellow wallpaper, a two-gallon saucepan in the fireplace. Moustaches twitched at the smell. Beyond, they looked into the kitchen (another two-gallon saucepan) and the scullery (a tin bath); in the bedroom, on the unmade double bed were a pile of bloody clothes, a kitchen cloth, a saw.

'See this?' Skinner said, indicating the saw. 'Skin and blood.'

On the other side of the bed were a brown fibre trunk and a hat-box. Skinner looked at Sir Bertram. They crossed to the trunk, Sir Bertram lifted the lid.

'Oh, my Christ . . .' Skinner said under his breath. They looked down at the large chunks of bloody flesh with sawn-through bone-ends. 'Human?'

'Undoubtedly . . . a breast . . . ribs . . . this looks like a piece of a . . . yes, of . . . a pelvis . . . What's this?' Sir Bertram reached into the trunk. It was a square white-metal biscuit tin stamped *Meecher's Tea-Time Favourites. 2lb Size. Jubilee Assortment*. He met the blue kippers-and-tea gaze, raised the lid. 'Yes, I see . . . small bowel . . . neck of uterus . . . an ovary . . .

Skinner did not look. Carefully, Sir Bertram replaced the lid, laid the tin aside, glanced at Skinner whose Adam's apple was rising and falling. 'Anything in the hat-box, Detective Chief Inspector? Maybe the head?' Skinner stood back, gave Sir Bertram precedence. Coolly, from the hat-box, between finger and thumb, Sir Bertram lifted out three, four items of bloody clothing, a fifth . . . Underneath were more hunks of flesh. 'Muscle and skin here . . . lower abdominal area it looks like . . . pubic hair is that? . . . looks as if he's boiled all this.'

'Boiled it? What for?'

'Feeding.'

Skinner cleared his throat. 'You mean – ?'

'To animals.'

'Female, at any rate?'

'Yes. At least one, fair-haired female. Can't tell you anything more yet. I shall have to examine it all, see what's here.'

They went back to the evil-smelling lounge. Sir Bertram bent over a saucer by the hearth.

'What is it?'

'Solidified fat. Could be human.' He peered into a big saucepan on the fire. 'Reddish liquid . . . thick layer of grease on top. That's probably where he's been boiling it.' Sir Bertram opened his bag and began changing – long white apron, artificial shirtsleeves, rubber gloves. 'Now, Detective Chief Inspector, I shall need a table, the one from the kitchen will do. If you would get the trunk and hat-box in here I shall be obliged, and the tin; and, if I might have his services, Sergeant Nichols – kindly ask him to take notes as I dictate. Don't let anybody touch the fireplace, I need all the cinders and ash. Oh, and Detective Chief Inspector, careful where you are standing, isn't that a bloodstain on the carpet . . .?'

The two parts of the pelvic cavity fitted together pretty well, the pubococcygeus had been cut through, the perineal membrane and urogenital diaphragm were incomplete. On the left-hand portion, he traced with his eye the course of the medial femoral circumflex and the profunda femoris . . . the sartorius and the adductor longus had both been severed just above the femoral artery, and the lower part of the limb was missing. A portion of the bulbospongiosus remained. He had obviously divided her with the saw upwards, evidently to eliminate the uterus first. The only trace of the uterus was the neck which had been cut through. The right-hand portion also had a stump of femur and flesh adhering.

He looked up and saw with some surprise that the blinds of the mortuary room had paled; the traffic noise from below had increased. He had reconstituted the right half of the chest to the twelfth vertebra, most of the ribs and right breast, a piece of the right lung adhering to the chest wall.

In the next room he heard Baker, the head mortuary assistant, open the outer door, speak to somebody outside; Baker knew better than to disturb him; he looked at his watch; 8.46. He straightened up, allowed himself a brief pause, contemplating the headless half-built cadaver, then turned away from the slab, reached out and let the blind up with a slap. The sun showed thinly through the veering clouds but the rain had stopped some time ago; the roofs and roadway were beginning to dry out. The phone in the outer room went and a moment later Baker knocked on the door and put his head in. 'Good morning, Sir Bertram, Detective Inspector Skinner would like a word with you.'

'Detective Chief Inspector.'

'Oh, yes. Sorry.'

Sir Bertram went through.

'Sir Bertram? I was wondering if you had any news for me?'

'I still have a great deal to do but I think I can tell you there was only one woman. No duplicates.'

'Then could we hope to have a report soon, Sir Bertram?'

'My dear Skinner, there were – how many? – forty-five separate pieces in the hat-box alone – and I have yet to reconstruct the abdominal area. I've been working all night; there are parts missing and I have to sift through all that ash and cinder. You must let me do this in my own way.'

'I don't want to hurry you, Sir Bertram . . . Any indication of how he killed her?'

'Nothing on the parts I have but I need a closer examination. She was well-built, rather big, fair-haired, twenty-five to thirty-five I would say. You haven't found the head yet?'

'If we can believe him, sir, we shan't. He made a statement early this morning. He's been having an affair with her, going on for several months. She was a clerk in the West End named Mabel Maynard. He says she followed him down to Lynford, they had a row and a scrap, she fell down and stunned herself on the fireplace, he says; he's not sure if he didn't strangle her in the struggle. All events, when he found she was dead, he panicked, cut her up. Burnt her head on the fire, boiled some of the parts, managed to throw others away.'

'I see. I'm sure you'll find he was always a great favourite with the ladies.'

'As a matter of fact, Sir Bertram, from what everybody says, that's exactly what he was.'

Anticipation began at the narrow concrete walk dividing the front lawn of the Public Library, continued up the steps into the entrance where she grasped the harp-shaped brass door-handle to heave the door open, and burst with a small delicious plop as she encountered the mingled fragrance of heated cast-iron steam radiators, floor-wax and Leo's pipe.

The woman library assistant inside glanced up, instantly looked away. Modestly, Ivy laid the books she was returning for inspection and, when the woman, whose mouth had contracted, had released the little wicket-gate, passed through. She was careful not to seem in the least eager, sauntered, hand brushing her skirt, past the row of books just returned, picked one out, put it back. At this time of the afternoon, except Thursdays, the Library was deserted and of course she avoided Thursdays. She advanced slowly towards the main stacks, turned as if at random out of the woman's view. The frosted glass door of Leo's office was open and as she appeared he rose from his desk, laid down his pipe and came smilingly out to her. Fleetingly they touched hands.

'Hello, my dear. How are you?' He bent forward, attentively gallant, a touch of the captain just back from the trenches, and for a second she thought he was going to kiss her fingertips. 'I've been looking forward to seeing you so much.'

'Leo . . .'

'I've got a nice selection for you.'

They had been on first-name terms for two weeks now and seemed to have known each other for much longer than a couple of months. It was his maturity that pleased her so much, his serious reliability, the gentlemanly, manicured charm that made one forget his lack of . . . well . . . conventional good looks, because, seen from a certain angle in the right light, his face was interesting. Of course, his limp – he had not exactly got it at the front but she always imagined he had; she had plodded beside his stretcher holding his grateful hand through the churned mud of Ypres for two hours and the General, as he had passed in his staff car, had saluted. She was sure his gallantry with her, his well-bred attentiveness, made other people think of him as a wounded officer too. In any event, she had never liked men with jutting chins; Leo's small reddish moustache showed his sensitivity, she thought, and his glasses and sparse hair produced an almost – well – dome-like suggestion and added to his professional look. Moreover, it counted greatly in his favour that, unlike too many men nowadays, Leo had not had much experience with the fair sex; though he was always eager to please them, he was always the perfect gentleman.

He tilted towards a bookshelf where he had set out a half-dozen books, but before they looked at them Ivy said, 'Oh, wait a minute . . . something I saw the other day in the paper . . . what was the name . . . Yes, Madam Bovair, I think . . . Is that good?'

'Madam . . .? I don't think I . . .? Oh yes, I see . . . M'mm, well, I don't think . . . I wouldn't if I were you, my dear. Not quite your style. No, definitely not. Foreign, you know . . . French. In fact, he got into serious trouble with it, the author, even in France. Prosecuted. There was a full-scale trial. Yes. That'll give you an idea.' He nodded. 'Have a look at these.'

In the silence the radiators ticked. She turned her eyes to him, their fingers entwined. (The tragedy of his last night of leave before the Big Push hung over them, but they bravely smiled.)

'Couldn't we share an evening together at the theatre, my dear? There are some splendid things on in the West End this season.'

It always sounded so smart when he spoke like that . . . especially the 'share an evening' . . . such taste and breeding; it was his first definite proposal that they should go up to Town together; hitherto they had only crossed the local Common one afternoon. And the West End!

'Well . . . I'd love to but . . . It's, you see . . . I . . .'

Another borrower, a shapeless elderly man in a grey gabardine, shuffled into view. They moved apart, Ivy bent over the row of books, looking absorbed. Keble Howard . . . Winifred

32

Graham: *The Beautiful Mrs Leach* . . . Marjorie Bowen: *The Two Carnations* . . . Paul Trent: *The Unexpected Daughter* . . . Madame Albanesi: *The Courage of Love* . . . Bertha Clay: *A Woman's Temptation.*

'I think you'd like the Albanesi,' Leo softly said. 'Or have you read *Brook Evans* by Susan Glaspell? A ripping book. Or what about a Stern . . .?'

Slowly the elderly borrower oozed away.

'Some of the performances start quite early,' Leo said.

'Well, you see, it's . . . it's really Boudie. I . . .'

'But it wouldn't be . . . I mean . . . I hope you don't think I meant . . .'

'No . . . I . . . Let's think about it.'

He moved a few steps away, bobbed down to see the Library clock, came back. 'I could leave in about half an hour, ask Miss Chitty to lock up when it's time. If we could walk back together?'

'Yes,' she smiled and nodded. 'I'll go up to the Reading Room and look at some magazines in the meantime. I'll take the Albanesi.'

3

The senior police moustache saluted. A patter of recognition like a little shower of applause, perhaps simply a minute explosion of labials, skipped across the crowded courtroom as Sir Bertram Pendleton moved to his place, giving one nod to Sir Henry Hay-Orpington, Crown Counsel. He sat alone, apart from the others as usual, and placed his black bag at his feet. The cylinder of his tall collar separated his head at the top from his tie at the bottom; he sat upright, two extended fingers of his right hand entwined in the opening of his black waistcoat, austere, confident, judiciously at ease. No one spoke to him – no one would. Redpath, Dugald and the other medical men on the Defence side, he ignored. Carstick KC avoided even a glance.

Hay-Orpington's triple chin quivered – a bullfrog on a lilypad digesting a fly; abruptly his adhesive tongue flipped out, struck a gnat on the prisoner's cheek, snapped back. Sir Bertram's eye on the prisoner noted the same quiet pudgy-faced composure he had observed in the Magistrate's Court. Admirable attention to the hair, thick black brilliantined hair, exquisitely parted, brushed and glossed, a high Valentino gloss; dark suit, breast-pocket handkerchief, dark tie. A young man of eminently good character, Band of Hope, Sunday-School teacher, regular church-goer, assiduous student of the Bible, on which, perhaps, his thoughts had run with quiet reverence while he sawed off the girl's head in the middle of the night. Sir Bertram's lips tightened imperceptibly at the thought of Brilliantino contending with his experience, his mastery, his art.

'The court! . . .'

A clog-dance of boots knocking, standing up. Little old dried-up Adie, walnut and candle-grease under his wig.

'John William Pearson, you stand charged upon this indictment, with murder, that is to say on 7 November, 1931 at Rooksby in this County, you murdered Edna Mildred Selby. Are you guilty or not guilty?'

'Not guilty, my Lord.'

Hay-Orpington stuck his hand into the back of his robe, strutted, twisted, wheeled, setting out the case. '. . . So that by early November this was the position. Edna Mildred Selby, believing she was pregnant by Pearson, was urging him to marry her at once; but realizing that Pearson was cooling towards her, was in fact attracted by another woman, had decided that she must press matters to a conclusion. On 7 November she came down to have things out, to hold Pearson to his promises. After that day, nobody except the Prisoner saw Miss Selby alive . . .'

Hay-Orpington flapped his robe . . . the police inquiries . . . the finding of the girl's body buried in the wood near the Prisoner's small-holding.

'The body was examined by Sir Bertram Pendleton, the eminent pathologist, whose reputation I imagine no one in this court will question.' (A glance, a pause, as if to stress the absurdity of the thought.) 'Sir Bertram was able to say quite positively – quite definitely – that the body showed nothing, no evidence at all, to suggest that Miss Selby had tried to hang herself as Pearson had told the police. On the other hand, Sir Bertram did find extensive bruising on the girl's face, head and body, most it caused just before death. The jury will hear Sir Bertram explain his findings. If, after that, they are satisfied that the Prisoner's story is lies from start to finish, they will have no doubt that this unfortunate girl was badly beaten before her death.

'And what if Pearson really had come back and found her hanging? Why not cut her down and call for help at once? Would that not be the natural thing? He did not do so. Because, I submit, he had beaten her so severely that he had killed her. So he cut her up and buried her . . .'

The succession of nervous witnesses, their awed faces, bul-

36

bous eyes, a goitre . . . Hay-Orpington reading the girl's idiotic letters – mustn't say idiotic, 'pathetic' the papers would say, the Great British Press; so depressing! As usual, Sir Bertram Pendleton tingled with longing for subversion . . . as soon as he opened his bag, the white Leghorn cock sprang out, strutted slowly, jerkily with dainty high-raised steps across the floor of the court, halting in mid-movement, twisting its head, claw poised. 'Officer – remove that bird!' Sir Bertram bent down and drew a white skipping-rope from the bag, skipped a one-two-three, a twirl at the side, cross-hands and through the loop. The white rope flashed.

'Sir Bertram Pendleton! . . . ' What? . . . The voice . . . ah, yes . . . he was being called. He rose, stepped confidently forward, shoulders back, catching the usual murmurs of appreciation.

Hay-Orpington was all deference. The usual introduction, Sir Bertram's official position, his eminence, his unequalled experience and so on. Sir Henry bowing to Sir Bertram, Sir Bertram just perceptibly bowing back, a knightly exchange of gallantries; what ordinary juryman could doubt that they knew the truth? Two Sirs make a right.

They performed an elaborate *pas de deux* among the bruises on the body, the sites, the sizes, damage to underlying tissue. 'I have no doubt that they were all caused just before death,' Sir Bertram said.

Mr Justice Adie perched forward. 'No question in your opinion, Sir Bertram?'

'No doubt at all, my Lord. All caused just before death.'

An audible gasp came from Redpath and the others on the Defence bench. Sir Bertram lifted his chin. Proceeding, Hay-Orpington passed to the Prisoner's claim that the girl had hanged herself in his absence.

'I found nothing to support that – no marks of a rope, no damage to the neck. She had two natural creases across the front of her neck like most women, but they had nothing to do with hanging. She died from shock due to being beaten. It was the combined effect of the beating and severe bruising.'

Two reporters went out. *Fatal Beating. Sir Bertram in Box. Sir Bertram Pendleton told the Old Bailey jury today that Edna Selby did*

37

not hang herself but died as a result of a beating. 'There is no doubt about it,' Sir Bertram said.

Carstick, as usual, weaved with his chin down. If the girl had been beaten as severely as Sir Bertram Pendleton had said, 'with very great violence,' surely some of the bones, especially in the face, would have been broken? At least the skin would have been?

Cool, upright, buttonhole perkily pointing, Sir Bertram put him right. No, no. No bones or skin broken.

Wasn't that surprising?

'No.'

What about other injuries such as a woman protecting herself might receive? Injuries to hands, shoulders, or arms?

'No, nothing,' Sir Bertram said.

'Well, now, if you take a heavy cudgel like this one, which the Prisoner kept for self-defence and which my learned friend has suggested may have been used to beat the girl – if this were used with murderous violence on the girl, would it produce bruises without breaking the skin?'

'Oh certainly. It depends on the part of the body.'

'Accepting murderous violence, wouldn't you really expect to find broken skin and bones? Particularly on the face?'

'No. It would only break skin and bone on some parts, directly on the cheek-bone for instance, but not on others.'

Sometimes Carstick pumped gently with upturned palm as if weighing something in it, a snowball or mud pie he was itching to throw. Sir Bertram jauntily flexed a knee; he enjoyed blocking Carstick.

'Would you exclude the possibility that the girl tried to hang herself, lost consciousness in the process while still alive, but died of shock immediately after she was cut down?'

'Oh definitely. Definitely exclude that.'

If a neurotic overwrought girl tried to hang herself she could die from shock? No, no. Sir Bertram couldn't accept that. No-o, no.

The furrows on Carstick's brow deepened. Why had Sir Bertram not used a microscope when he first examined the girl's neck?

'Because it was not necessary. There was nothing abnormal

to see, with or without a microscope.'

'You simply relied on the naked eye?'

'Yes. If I had noticed any slight abnormality, I would have used the microscope; but there was no point in doing so.' If Carstick had expected to fluster him with this, he had miscalculated. Sir Bertram allowed himself a minute humorous pursing of the lips.

Put in Adie: 'You were quite satisfied, Sir Bertram, that there was nothing abnormal?'

'Nothing abnormal at all.'

Rustles of approval as Carstick sat down. Hay-Orpington steered up like a tug-boat. 'How many hanged persons have you seen in the course of your career, Sir Bertram?'

'Many, many hundreds.'

'Many hun-dreds . . . ' Hay-Orpington's eyebrows rose in mock appreciation. 'What did you find here?'

'I examined the neck with particular care because of the statement that the girl had hanged herself. I made numerous incisions in the neck but found no sign of a haemorrhage, no mark of a rope, no reddening. There was no point, therefore, in making microscopic slides. At the second post-mortem examination, by Dr Redpath and Mr Dugdale, after the body had been exhumed, the neck tissues were too far gone in decomposition for any examination with a microscope or without one to be of any use.'

'Thank you, Sir Bertram.'

He stepped down, resumed his seat, twiddled his buttonhole, put his nose to it appreciatively. The reporters for the *Star* and the *Evening Standard* left to phone in the end of his evidence. No doubt he would be called again but for the moment Carstick was flattened. They were calling the next witness. 'Police Constable Potts . . .'

Slowly the court darkened, they switched the lights on, the reporters came and went, the court stenographer was relieved. Mr Justice Adie's wig, much too big, seen from below where Sir Bertram sat, rested on the bench like an upturned vase, a glass bell, a cheese bell over the wrinkled face, the old man's chin pitted with small holes and crevasses of collapsed flesh, or perhaps merely blackheads, the outlines crumbling in

bluish streaks and patches into a Stilton, perhaps a blue Glouc-
ester or Wensleydale, a crack below like a mouth breathing
corruption, an exhibit in a superior grocer's shop where they
had sawdust on the floor . . . He crumbled his jaws.

At last, 'If that is all, Sir Henry, I think we can adjourn,' Adie
said. 'Tomorrow morning. Ten-thirty.'

Sir Bertram pulled on his raincoat.

'Pardon, Sir Bertram.'

'Sergeant?'

'If I was you I'd go out by the side door. There's a crowd
waiting to watch you leave. Just down the corridor, Sir Bertram. Constable here will show you the way.'

Ivy folded the paper with the familiar picture on the front
page. 'The *News* calls you the star witness.'

'H'm.'

'The *Star* says something about Mr Carstick making you
admit a slip-up . . . what was it, no microscopic examination of
. . . I think something . . .?'

'Slip-up! What bosh. Examination of the girl's neck. I told
him it wasn't necessary.'

'But can you imagine that young man cutting her up in that
shed?'

'Brilliantino? He's as cool as custard.'

'Mrs Tickner says the defence has got an array of senior
medical men against you.'

'Redpath and Co – they're on tomorrow. You'll see . . .
Ha-ha-ha!'

Quickly Ivy's hand turned down the dial on her hearing aid.
She said softly 'Don't laugh like that Boudie. You make me
frightened.'

'H-ha-ha! Nothing to be frightened of, my dear.' He leaned
forward, squeezed her hand. 'What's that you've got out – the
book? Oh . . . romantic!'

Ivy always prepared an ample breakfast when he was giving
evidence at the Old Bailey – this morning it was porridge, two

kippers, toast and Oxford marmalade. He was in court for the opening. Redpath, called in mid-morning, glided to the box with a flap of his pudgy hand. Sir Bertram sat with fingertips joined expressing rigour, prepared to enjoy Redpath's exuberant excess . . . and defeat. As usual, Carstick reeled off a list of Redpath's posts and qualifications and Redpath complacently swayed. Tight waves of yellow hair lapped down over one side of his head above the plump rosy face.

In answer to Carstick's second question, Redpath launched into a voluble explanation of the circulatory system and Carstick had to pull him back. After the exhumation, when both he and Sir Bertram Pendleton had examined a sample of neck tissue under the microscope, he had seen some blood that had leaked out of the veins. 'That was evidence that a rope had been round the neck.'

Sir Bertram pursed his lips. To Adie, who represented the principle of dryness, desiccation, or rather the process of mummification, the drying-out of damp, a jelly like Redpath was deplorable. Adie's wig had a greenish tinge in the morning light . . . Mr Justice Stilton had changed into a mildewed cauliflower.

Redpath was saying, 'Sir Bertram Pendleton says he can tell that certain bruises were made just before death. You cannot distinguish between immediate ante- and post-mortem bruises. Nobody can . . . As for that cudgel which Sir Bertram says could have been used on the girl, that cudgel used with murderous violence would have smashed the skull like a . . . like . . . like an eggshell.'

In spite of himself, Sir Bertram began to feel the familiar irritation; his cheeks prickled, he felt the small nervous ticking somewhere along the abdominal aorta. But Hay-Orpington was rising to cross-examine. 'Sir Bertram Pendleton is the greatest living expert in forensic medicine, is he not?'

'I have heard some people say that.' Redpath's fingertips did a small exasperated dance on the edge of the witness-box.

'You agree?'

'That he has been so described, yes.'

'The expert who has had the greatest experience in medical-legal work?'

41

'Not more than I have.'

Redpath, that blusterer, daring to compare himself! Sir Bertram sat listening while Hay-Orpington dragged Redpath into a barbed-wire entanglement of argument over the marks on the girl's neck and, having cast doubt on Redpath's description, strongly suggested that they were just natural folds.

Bristled Redpath: 'That is not accurate!'

The bruises produced a regular flare-up. 'I repeat, it is impossible for the greatest expert to say if the bruises were caused just before or after death.'

'Do you question Sir Bertram Pendleton's findings?'

'I say nobody can decide. It is a common source of error.'

Hay-Orpington puffed himself up. 'You suggest that Sir Bertram Pendleton, whom you yourself agree is the greatest living pathologist, has made a common error?'

'I say she did not die from the bruises I saw.'

'But neither does Sir Bertram. He says she died of shock after the bruises. You are not trying to help me.'

'I am supposed to be explaining and clarifying medical findings not helping to win a case.'

'You contest Sir Bertram Pendleton's findings that she died from shock as a result of the bruises?'

'Yes. In my opinion, she died from shock as a result of an attempt to hang herself. I have seen it before, a man attempting to hang himself and dying before he could tie the second knot. Every medical student knows –'

'We are not medical students, Dr Redpath. We are here –'

'I must finish my answer, Sir Henry – every medical student knows the famous case of the nervous college caretaker who was laid on a mock guillotine and flicked across the neck with a wet towel – and died at once.'

'But that is mere hearsay, Dr Redpath, is it not? You were not a witness?'

'No. But you asked Sir Bertram Pendleton for instances –'

'Sir Bertram only spoke of cases from his own experience.' Whereupon, having Redpath on the defensive, Hay-Orpington easily muddled him up with questions about slides, skull thicknesses, slipknots, until Redpath, stung, said angrily, 'If I may say so, Sir Henry, you want things put in black and white, and in medicine there is usually a whole range of tones in between. In any event, an autopsy doesn't necessarily tell you how a person died.'

'Sir Bertram Pendleton has no doubt. Evidently you have, Dr Redpath.'

Sir Bertram caught Adie's expression as Redpath stepped down – disposed of! Dugald followed Redpath's general line. The girl's skull would not have withstood a blow from the cudgel. Lindsay Grey was equally positive. Altogether a different bird, Lindsay Grey, quiet, saturnine, a lot of darkish grey hair, thick eyebrows, eyes hidden in the sockets, a heavy shadow over the shaving area. 'I have been looking at slides like these for thirty years, practically daily. What you see on them is blood that leaked out when the girl tried to hang herself. Any competent laboratory worker can demonstrate it in two minutes. As to the bruises, they're of no consequence, nothing more than a St John's Ambulance first-aid man sees after any weekend rugger match.'

Said Adie: 'How do you explain that, after the exhumation, when Sir Bertram Pendleton examined the neck tissue under a microscope, he saw no leaked blood and you and Dr Redpath did?'

'The rope round her neck did not break all the bloodvessels, only some. If you took fifty samples from the same part, only a few might show blood. Dr Redpath got a sample with blood, Sir Bertram Pendleton got one without.'

The court stirred. Sir Bertram sat doodling on a PM form. They were all against him. He was recalled. He strode to the witness-box with expectant relish.

'What the other doctors have described as haemorrhage in the skin of the neck are simply the remains of sebaceous glands. There is no evidence at all that the girl was hanged.'

Said Adie: 'So that you suggest the other doctors may have been mistaken?'

'Have been mistaken.'

A muffled reverential organ-note from the courtroom . . . did he hear a half-stifled cheer? Adie called an adjournment. Redpath and the others trooped out, talking together. As Sir Bertram turned away to avoid them, Rogers, the court clerk, came up. 'If you'd care to wait in the little room next to my office, as usual, Sir Bertram?'

'Thank you, Rogers.'

Demolished them all; they wouldn't get a look in! Twirling a Charlie Chaplin walking-stick, he slithered across the room on a fish-tail splay. They all came back for the summing-up. Sir Bertram observed that Adie's bottom lip stuck out, not a good sign for Carstick.

'Gentlemen of the jury, learned Counsel on both sides in this anxious case have put every point to you with the utmost . . .' Sir Bertram dozed lightly until he came to the medical evidence. 'You will carefully consider Dr Redpath's evidence . . . As to Sir Bertram Pendleton, his professional eminence is well known – that has never been disputed by the Defence, in particular by Dr Redpath . . . without doubt, Dr Bertram's opinion is the very best, most expert, opinion that can be obtained and you will give the utmost care and consideration to what he said . . .'

Carstick made a note; Redpath and the others looked huffed. The moment the last juryman had gone out, Sir Bertram picked up his bag and made his way through the back corridor.

'Call you a taxi, Sir Bertram?'

'No thank you, Constable. I'll walk,' and his buoyancy made him add, 'just to St Edward's.' It was almost a confidence, a show of fellow-feeling.

'Right you are, sir.' The constable looked as if he had received a crisp Bradbury.

At the bottom of the hospital steps, when Sir Bertram emerged two and a half hours later, the newspaper vendor was calling out, 'Late Nigh Finoo . . . Murdurvurdic . . . Murdurvurdic . . .' Sir Bertram did not unfold his copy until he was in the train. Jury only out half an hour. Guilty, naturally.

The bedroom wardrobe mirror, slightly loose, reflected the image of Sir Bertram Pendleton in tutu, blue socks and suspenders. Hands on hips, he bent his knee, lifting his right foot from the floor, pointed the foot downwards and twirled it in a circular motion. His palms touched the white tutu. Soaring in an *entrechat*, he landed with feet at quarter to three on Adie's bench, sat on Adie's head, squashing the wig . . . the court staff and police nodded in unison. The white cock crowed. Sir Bertram fluffed the tutu.

Softly the door opened and Ivy put her head in; her hair was done in earphones tonight. 'Boudie, dear . . . don't you think . . .?'

His mouth widened, he thrust his neck out, showing bright red celluloid gums and protruding teeth.

'I wish you'd come down . . . Are you sure you don't want any supper? I've got such a nice piece of haddock . . . really, you mustn't excite yourself like this . . . come along, dear . . . No, not in the tutu . . . not tonight, there's a dear, I'm afraid Mrs Tickner might come in . . . Will you, Boudie?' She was anxious, gentle, pleading. 'Please take those teeth out, they frighten me.'

Sir Bertram lay across the bed, motionless, mouth open, eyes shut, prostrate. The wardrobe glass reflected, on the far side of the room, a segment of the yellow and green head and one beautiful luminous glass eye of Roddy Rockinghorse.

4

Ivy laid Madame Albanesi on the hall-stand where a caller would see it (a distinguished cosmopolitan touch) and remembered that the Library would be open later tomorrow and she would be able to linger and walk home with Leo . . . or halfway home, since they were careful not to chance a meeting with Boudie. In the front room she sat down by the gas fire, allowing herself her little afternoon islet with a Player's No 3, hoping that Mrs Tickner wouldn't pop in. She and Boudie, instead of keeping the front room shut up, inhabited only by the best furniture, used it like any other, every day – another sign of genuine social standing, which Mrs Tickner, for instance, wouldn't understand.

Her upward glance was jogged by the slightly disordered arrangement of the mantelshelf (Mrs Tickner vulgarly called hers the 'mantelpiece'), then . . . oh yes!, the new item, the photograph of them all in the garden that she had brought down yesterday. It looked so well, Father in dark jacket and fashionable cream waistcoat, once again gazing off left as if some marauder had at the last second surprised his attention, Mother, rather Victorian, a general bulge, a black ribbon in her hair, long-waisted tunic and full ground-length skirt, Bertram on one side, herself next to Mother and dear, departed George, tallest of all in his RFC uniform, beside her. It expressed splendidly the eternal verities on which Father and Mother had founded all their lives, the moral superiority of the great English upper class, supported and confirmed, as Father always explained, by religion and the monarchy, its ideals of restraint and respectability. Boudie looked particularly jaunty and at ease, far above the common run, one hand in jacket pocket, the other holding Girlie on her leash. A family of substance, obviously. The annoying flash of recollection – Mrs Tickner who had once seen the photograph saying they all looked decidedly – well – it was quickly gone, gone at once, absolutely; why *strange*, in any event?

Her gaze rested on dear Boudie. In reality (it was their little secret), she knew he longed to . . . to . . . well, yes, to shake, to upset those cherished ideals . . . well, not really, but just in fun . . . in his own way . . . that he was – what was that phrase she'd read somewhere the other day about somebody? . . . she'd forgotten . . . quite appropriate, she'd thought at the time – oh yes, 'just keeping the lid on,' that was it. Boudie, just keeping the lid on. All through those earlier years, though he had never spoken openly to her of it, she knew that he had secretly hated being forced into medicine by Father; it had been something Father had expected, was thus ordained, Boudie had silently bowed to it and, never aspiring to dazzle, had finally taken his B.Sc. at thirty. But it had unsettled him. Oh yes, yes . . .

But then he had come round . . . so peculiar the way things worked out . . . So that it didn't even seem strange now that he should have begun by resisting what soon absorbed his life . . . didn't seem strange to her, at all events, perhaps because Boudie was inconceivable somehow in any other role.

Dear Boudie, she wished he had friends . . . any friends . . . friends she could talk to about him, who would be jolly with him, jolly him along, teach him to relax and enjoy himself. He never seemed able to do that. Even his assistants, the men he worked closely with, never got to know him, she was sure of that . . . the way they spoke of him, the distance they kept. Such a pity that his friendship with pale, pale, thin Madge Holford hadn't ripened a long neck into something more; they had never actually been engaged, though after six years it had sometimes seemed they might get to that. And since then he had never shown any interest in anyone else.

She wished he had a hobby or took recreation . . . but no. Father had made him a member of that club, the Junior something, for appearance's sake but he never went there, disliked

48

the place. He worked too hard – his whole life was spent in the laboratory or in the coroners' courts or with the police or travelling round the country doing autopsies or giving evidence.

She sighed, put out her cigarette. Of course, it had all made it harder for her. There was Leo now . . . and she was afraid of Leo ending as RM had ended. She had truly loved RM – oh dear, who – he saw! – his Scots accent, his distinguished aquiline nose, his distinguished manners, his distinguished position in the engineering profession. With a delicious inner plunge she passed into that moment on RM's knee . . . a warm hand reaching the skin between the stocking top and under the elastic right up to – the evening Boudie, oh dear! had burst unexpectedly into the room . . . he saw! . . . I hope he . . . hand . . . stocking top . . . and RM had swiftly withdrawn his hand from under . . . facing the door too! . . . and she knew Boudie had seen. Even after all this time, the flush tingled her cheeks. RM would have taken her with him, a great white liner, explosions of palms and red mountains to South Africa . . . but how could she leave Boudie?

She had promised Mother solemnly always to look after Boudie, *always* . . . yes, Mother, yes . . . Mother lying in bed still wearing her velvet neckband and all her rings, her own rings, her Mother's rings, lifting a hand to make her promise, fingernails like bits of polished shell, her fingers the bright-coloured sticky pastries she used to buy at the pastry-cook's, ruby-studded éclairs, emerald-and-icing gateaux, platinum petits-fours with sapphires and pistachio icing.

But Boudie, after that evening, had hated RM, had kept questioning her about him, well after RM had gone. It would be so hard to explain to Leo, dear, gallant, patient Leo wielding his Webley, leading his men over the top with a wide beckoning arm-sweep, his Sam Browne belt glinting in the watery morning light.

All sorts of feelings began to creep into Ivy, she felt the gathering excitement of an upswing.

49

'I rang you up about four but they said there was no–'

'I had to pop out,' Ivy said from the dining-room. 'My library book had expired so I had to return it.' Hastily she added, 'It did look for a minute as if it would stop this afternoon.'

Sir Bertram Pendleton by the fire continued taking off his wet spats.

'Anyway, dear,' Ivy said, changing the subject, 'it was a nice idea of yours for a surprise.'

He had done something for the first time, brought home a flagon of Emu Brand Genuine Australian Burgundy-type wine for dinner, and in consequence Ivy had laid the table with one of Mother's best openwork table cloths and put out their stem glasses. Passing the off-licence by the station he had caught the rich glow of the advertisement and, thinking of the trip north he must start in the morning, had gone in on impulse, wondering at himself once he was inside, and bought it. Fortunately, to the prematurely bald young man in a bow tie behind the counter, his face was a blank.

The folding doors were open to allow the gas fire in the front room to take the chill off. 'Mrs Tickner's always saying she finds the house like ice but I don't think so,' Ivy said.

'Perfectly all right.' Sir Bertram rose. 'Now you sit down, my dear, I'll do the rest.' He went into the kitchen and came back with the supper dish, silver-plated cover and carving knife. Ivy looked up from arranging her napkin on her lap, took the cover off and gave a small stifled shriek. A foot. 'Oh . . . Boudie! Really!' Sir Bertram bared a half-inch of teeth, his long face dourly pleated.

'Uhh . . . Uhh . . . Big tt-toe, my dear? Or will you have a little . . . uhh . . . uhh . . .

'No, take it away. You're awful . . .'

'The sweet meat nestling round the cuboid and navicular –?'

'Take it *away*! Boudie!'

Pleated no longer, he picked it up and carried it out, came back with the cold beef.

'I should have thought you'd got tired of those old jokes,' she said.

'But you're always surprised!' He pursed his lips. 'Never mind, have some Emu.' He poured the wine. 'Don't throw it away, the foot, I mean. I need it.'

Supper proceeded as usual, without much talk. They had never been a family for useless chatter.

'What time's your train?' Ivy asked. 'In the morning.'

'Eight-ten.'

'The Railway Hotel, as usual?'

'At Darlington, yes. Then I go to Durham, Stockport . . . I'll leave you the list. Walker will know, of course, he'll be in touch with you. And I'll give you a call every evening.'

They ate in silence for a while, then Ivy said, 'Mrs Tickner says there's some dust-up about the Pearson case.'

'Dust-up?'

'That was what she . . . she used another word, what was it? Muttering . . . no murmurings . . . yes, murmuring, she said. She says people in the legal profession are complaining your word's become as good as law . . . you're a sort of . . . of oracle, never wrong, the judges think you are infallible – and that – and that, according to her, that's bad. They're calling you Saint Bertram.'

'The jury decides, my dear, not the judge.'

'Well, she says – I don't know where she got this – she says it's all wrong to expect a judgement on a medical matter from a jury. And she says . . . she says all the others, the other doctors, were against you; and the jury, they just followed you because you're the biggest man. I said to her, because you're the most thorough, most . . . not that ridiculous Dr Redpath, I said . . .'

'The jury were sensible people and Mrs Tickner's a fool.'

'That's what I said to her . . . words to that effect. How can she judge? I mean . . . And what's the point of bringing this up, too late now? What's the point? I don't think it's very friendly.'

'Don't let it upset you, my dear.' He reached across the table and took her hand. She smiled back, nervously touched her hearing aid.

'My things ready for the morning?' he said. 'Second trousers cleaned?'

'Yes, dear.'

Another silent pause. Ivy said, 'Where did you put my little cigarette-lighter?'

'I don't think I've seen it, my dear. The one I gave you?'

'Yes. I'm sure I saw you pick it up. You must have taken it. You've got it in your pocket – you were wearing that suit. Do look.'

Pendleton gazed at her; she had lost it and was short-circuiting a possible reproach from him. He recognized the familiar system.

'Why don't you tell me honestly, Boudie?' She was slightly flushed, a nervous tremor in one hand.

'Don't be anxious, my dear, we'll – In fact, now I think about it, you're quite right, I must have put it somewhere, moved it.' He was dipping into his waistcoat pockets. 'Use the old one for the time being. If it doesn't turn up, I'll get you a new one. I promise.' He smiled, touched her hand again. They resumed eating. Silence. She still wasn't entirely reassured. The knives and forks tapped on the plates; presently he looked up at her again. Ivy brought her gaze up to meet his and smiled. Pendleton took a sip of his wine. 'H'mm. Pleasant . . .'

'Lovely colour,' Ivy said.

'Body . . .'

The tension had gone. Presently when she had served his apple pie and custard, Ivy said, 'Is that – what was it? – Frost case one of them you're attending to this time?' and, at his continued frown, 'The young actor. The old aunt who died in the boarding-house fire where they were staying – West Hartlepool, wasn't it?'

'Oh . . . *Snow*. No, it's been adjourned. And she didn't die in the fire. He strangled her.'

'Oh Boudie, are you sure?'

The old woman's fat, heavy, inert body . . . too long, too long getting her settled, head on one side, mouth open, there . . . as if she got up and collapsed . . . empty bottle of port beside her, adjust its position with a little touch of his foot. Now, quick! across the room . . . sweating, push the pink and green chintz armchair nearer to the gasfire, there . . . no, not too close . . . there. Newspapers ready in the chair . . . tear the sheets apart, rumple them into a rough ball and stuff it underneath the chair. Now a match to the gasfire . . . pop! pop! He jumps back frightened as it snarls and roars. Why is it roaring

52

like that? Shaking . . . a flip of the hand, turns it off. He tries
again, drops the match into the grate; the fire burns normally.
Another match . . . he puts it to the newspapers under the
chair . . . the ball of paper won't light, too tight . . . he stabs
match after match at it. At length he pulls the ball of paper out,
loosens it, thrusts it back and manages to get a small flame to
curl. Upright he swings round. She was moving! . . . No . . .
Dare not move her again now. Too late. The webbing and
stuffing of the armchair begin to crackle and spit, giving out
smoke. On his knees he tries to peer under the chair to make
sure the paper is entirely burnt. The carpet begins to smoul-
der. He feels sick, his head is going round . . . At the door he
listens . . . nothing. Coughing . . . the room slowly becoming
grey with smoke. At last when he can stand it no longer, he
pulls the door open and runs into the passage.

'Of course I'm sure.'

'I see they've got Sir William Makepeace for the Defence,'
Ivy said.

'Snow will hang. A little more of that piecrust, dear, please.'

A cut from the lower end of the vertical incision, along the
pubic crest then neatly below the course of the inguinal ligament, extend the incision . . . to the anterior superior iliac
spine, there we are . . . and along the iliac crest. Carefully he
reflected the skin of the abdomen, paused . . . h'm, yes . . .
Right and left superficial epigastric veins and their anasto-
moses engorged. Obviously an obstruction of the inferior vena
cava. Result – superficial veins in the abdominal wall, particularly round the umbilicus, greatly dilated and tortuous. He
marked on his card *Caput Medusae*.

There was sometimes a moment when he became en-
tangled, when he could not determine whether the autopsy he
was performing with such queer inconclusiveness was the one
he had completed last night or a demonstration at the Central
Criminal Court before the Lord Chief Justice, the Appeal
Court, Princess Alice, the Old Bailey staff and distinguished
judges, all wearing silver-green toques. He would swim
vaguely, wake and recognize the hotel bedroom. 'Eh . . .?'

53

'Tea, sir. Seven o'clock.'

'Thank you.'

He worked for hours in the icy outdoor mortuary sheds – no drainage, feeble lighting, no storage for the cadavers. In the evenings, alone, he sat on the lumpy bed, beside Teddy, and wrote out his case-cards. 'Depressed fracture of skull from blunt instrument. Woman, aged about 32, 5' 6", long chestnut hair, thin, not well-fed. Fracture extends to base of skull with section of bone driven inward. Not pregnant, no ring, cheap cotton dress, black shoes . . .'

He was often tempted to have fun and 'improve' the evidence and twice added a harmless but mystifying detail which he explained with great aplomb to the awed coroner's jury, a brilliant cadenza. It rained daily, the sky was dark with soot. Somehow he always seemed to spend afternoons in slow trains, arriving among demonic chimneys in the dusk. Walker, the analyst, when they had to join forces, usually chose to stay at some pub or tavern – and in any event was no company. Without fail Sir Bertram telephoned Ivy each evening.

'Boudie, you forgot your galoshes. I've just found them. Really, you must –'

'Never mind. Are you all right, my dear?'

'Oh yes, perfectly all right. There's a letter for you from the Royal Free, one from the Scottish Office . . . some others that don't look important. That's all . . . Mrs Tickner's going away to Ventnor tomorrow for a couple of weeks, her old mother's not well, she says . . . Oh, yes Mr Piper rang up from the hospital but says it's nothing urgent.'

'Good. Have you had supper?'

'Yes. I wasn't really hungry so I just got a pattie from Sorby's. Now I'm going to listen to Sir Henry Wood.'

The repeated routine of the coroners' courts stunned him. 'My name is Bertram Pendleton, I am a pathologist . . . On 17 February I examined the body of the deceased . . . The liver was somewhat green in colour . . . ' Four and five times a day, sometimes, in the same court and the coroners insisted on going through the same rigmarole each time. 'My name is Bertram Pendleton, I am a pathologist . . . When Mr Forbes removed the lid of the coffin, I detected no smell except that of

54

the sawdust packed round the body. This, the sawdust, was clean and dry. The body, which was clothed in a long grey garment was moved . . . the wall of the abdomen was decidedly tight . . . some putrefactive gas had formed in the eyelids and under the skin of the breasts . . . There was a faint scar on the left of the chin and another at the base of the right thumb, both old scars . . . the cavity round the lungs contained a little red fluid . . . the lungs were deep red in colour and congested at the back . . .'

Most of the cases were suicides or accidents, he was no longer astonished by the fumbling local doctors. When he appeared they treated him as if, looking like the great undertaker-in-chief, he possessed some queer astrological knowledge of death.

'How many post-mortems do you do a year, Sir Bertram?'

'No idea,' he said, knowing that at the present rate it was about a thousand.

A vertical cut to open the descending part of the duodenum . . . push the probe through the wall of the bile duct into the lumen . . . verify the greater duodenal papilla . . . then into the duodenum. Pull out probe, pass it into the opening of the greater papilla and enter the hepatopancreatic ampulla . . . Left into the pancreatic duct . . .

Now and then a local doctor wanted to come and watch him; he insisted on silence, unless he was pointing something out. When he extracted an organ to weigh it in his hand, he occasionally passed it to the onlooker to judge the weight too. Once he had decided on the cause of death, he did not change his mind. His reputation flattened resentment of 'the London man'.

'In view of the peculiar circumstances, the family is not satisfied. We have heard that the deceased felt threatened. Inspector Biggs has testified that the police inquiries are still inconclusive. Yet you are confident, Sir Bertram, that he killed himself?'

'I have no doubt about it at all.'

'Why not?'

'From the obvious signs. Self-inflicted suicidal wounds may look like homicidal wounds; any suicidal wound may be imitated by a homicidal wound. Of course the reverse is not necessarily true – that any homicidal wound may be a suicidal one. But in this case the signs are clear. People who cut their throats invariably make a number of half-hearted superficial cuts first – in this case twelve. These cuts are usually high up on the neck, as here, on the left side if the person is right-handed, again as here, and vice versa. Then they make more determined, deeper cuts, almost always straight across the middle of the neck through the thyrohyoid ligament. Very frequently they deepen a cut already made and these deep cuts slope upwards towards the mouth, again as in this case.

'In a murderous attack you find none of these . . . these tentative cuts. The wounds are higher up and lower down on the neck, often run diagonally across. They slope backwards or downwards and you do not find the same wound cut into twice. In addition there are usually injuries to hands and forearms where the victim has tried to protect himself. None of these signs was present in this case.'

'Thank you, Sir Bertram. I am sure the jury are glad to have this eminent opinion. I . . . I confess I was inclined to ask the police to pursue their inquiries . . . but . . . ah . . . in view of your decided opinion, I shall direct the jury to bring in a verdict of suicide whilst of unsound mind.'

The hotel dining-rooms had their usual depressing effect.

'Try the weener snitzer, sir? Real nice. Sort of veal, I think, served with spaghetti and tomato sauce. Very popler.'

He knew the material conditions were atrocious, that he was overworking, paid nothing; but the narrowness and harshness echoed in his soul, forced him to conform, even perversely to enjoy it. Some obscure English notion endowed the rawness with virtue, made him cling to the surrounding mediocrity while hating it. It was as if all round him were bleakness up to the frontier of the brilliant gorgeous domain of his work. An invisible force held him to his routine; life reached its height in the exquisite feeling in a difficult case that he had the secret of what had happened. His relation with the cadaver was always full of poetic nuance, alive with exciting shifts and possibilities. Sometimes, in a flash of intuition, with a touch, a caress, he had the answer. With a single cut, calculated to a

56

millimetre, he could often see what had happened. And, now and then, his autopsy was a contest with the Sphinx . . . and even he could not solve the riddle – though he could say what the answer was *not*.

While he was bent over a cadaver in the freezing shack in his long apron, gloves and removable shirtsleeves, his physical and mental weariness dissolved, he worked without noticing the time, without any knowledge of the rest of life, his whole existence concentrated in the appearance of a vein, the deviation of a nerve, a delicately flushed centimetre of tissue. And lately there had been periods between autopsies for which he couldn't fill in details, when the images of trains and hotels and coroners' courts existed in a sort of mobile haze. It sometimes seemed to him that he had been doing post-mortems from time immemorial, that he was always, somehow or other, doing one, so that, when, in a distracted moment, his eye perceived a woman's elegant leg crossed in front of him in a railway carriage, some machinery at the back of his mind, without prompting, reviewed the anterior tibial artery and its ramifications, followed the course and connections of the perforating branch of the peroneal artery passing distal to the interosseous membrane, noting, in some cases that the perforating branch replaced the dorsalis pedis, though in most confirming that the dorsalis pedis continued the anterior tibial artery on to the dorsum of the foot, all of which, of course, was infinitely more beautiful than the sheen and contour of stocking and flesh. And the *posterior* rural compartment – even more promising to think of!

In the station buffet, sipping watery tea on the last day of the month, he read the *Chronicle's* preliminary report on the trial with which he was concluding this provincial visit.

MURDER TRIAL OPENS MONDAY
(picture Page One)

Sir Bertram Pendleton, the eminent pathologist, will be appearing in an unusual role when Douglas Ferguson of Murrayfield appears on trial for murder in the Edinburgh High Court on Monday. Sir Bertram, who has appeared as Crown witness in many murder trials south of the Border in recent years, will be giving evidence this time as witness for the Defence and will be assisted by Mr William Atkins, the well-known gunsmith of London. Ferguson, who has pleaded not guilty, is accused of murdering his wife Florence by shooting her in the head while she was writing at the kitchen table in their house in Murrayfield. Among other expert witnesses will be Dr Percy Redpath, the noted London pathologist, Dr Walter Pritchard and Dr Angus Moncrieff of Edinburgh and Dr Hamilton Weir of Glasgow. Ferguson is defended by Mr Duncan Currie KC.

They were sitting in the snug private bar of the Glenavon Hotel after the penultimate hearing.

'I wouldna' count on getting anything before the night train,' Pritchard said to Redpath. 'Won't have a verdict before sixish.'

'I was reckoning the Lord Advocate would finish tonight.'

'He'll have about another twenty minutes in the morning, wouldn't you think, Mr Muir?'

'Aye, about that. Then after Mr Currie there'll be a short adjournment before the Lord Justice Clark makes his charge to the jury.'

'Well, Pendleton's already left. He was telling the clerk as I came out.'

'Oh he never waits for the verdict. Sure of himself.'

'Young Ferguson's guilty as sin. He shot her all right.'

'Well, we all agree on that. But I'll take three to one he gets off.'

'I wouldn't have said so yesterday but I'm inclined to agree with ye tonight.'

'Once Pendleton said, "There is nothing inconsistent with the wound having been self-inflicted," it was all up.'

'But those tests of his were worth nothing!' Dr Wilfred Carr said with heat. 'It's as plain as day. The jury must have realized that.'

'Oh, I doubt that, my boy.'

'Well, I mean, he fires at a bit of cardboard in London – but uses a different gun and different ammunition. What's the good of that? As evidence? No validity. Then he comes up here, gets hold of the real gun, fires at cardboard and at human skin but *still* uses different ammunition. He gets a different result but oh, that doesn't disturb him a bit, he says it really amounts to the same thing. Doesn't in the least modify his London opinion.'

'I agree, but did you see the way the jury were watching him? Eh? Did ye? Dazzled, my boy! They thought he was speaking gospel. Sir Bertram Pendleton for the *Defence*? It's unheard of. You *have* to believe him!'

'He-he! If not, he could have been wrong in some of those murder cases south of the Border, where the fellow's been hanged – and then where are we all?'

'He had to admit that the test shots he fired in Edinburgh made more blackening on the skin than the ones he fired in London.'

'Oh, an important point, that blackening. Currie asks him if there's any real difference between the London and Edinburgh tests when it comes to rubbing the blackening off the skin, and he stands up there as cool as you like and says, "I should say not." And what do you think the jury understood by that? No difference between the tests – in other words, Pendleton is right.'

'Aye, that's certainly what they understood.'

'I thought the Lord Advocate had him cornered at one point: when he was saying, wasn't the important thing in these tests to use the same gun and the same ammunition? Oh, of course, says Pendleton – he could hardly deny it. So didn't he think that Pritchard's tests – after all they'd based the murder charge on Pritchard's tests – did he think Pritchard's tests with the same gun and the same ammunition, had more validity than his own? Oh no, says Pendleton. No . . .'

'Never gives an inch.'

'Always got an answer, thinks his own conclusions are indisputable.'

'I've been telling ye from the beginning, you're up against the pairsonality of the man.'

'Let's have a drop more of this Highland dew, gentlemen, and then I must go. Dinner appointment.'

5

It snowed lightly just before Easter. He had been present at two exhumations and performed twenty-six post-mortems in the same week. He was tired, he had developed an irritating tic, easing his neck in his collar, and he looked forward to getting home. On the telephone Ivy reported that all was well; Mrs Tickner, still in Ventnor, had telephoned about feeding her cat and, oh yes, she had started knitting a new cardigan for him, blue and burgundy, lovely colours.

He could hear the tea-kettle whistling in the background.

'You sound quite jolly.'

She laughed. 'I suppose it's knitting – always makes me feel cosy.'

'Well, I'll be with you tomorrow.' He put down the receiver and pushed open the door of the booth, somehow mysteriously not quite at ease; she had sounded unusually lively . . . yet . . .

From boyhood he had known that other people considered her a bit of a joke with her big-boned body, her Player's No 3, the succession of hearing aids which never worked properly, her readiness to be impressed with what was 'smart' and done in 'Society', her too-fair washed-out looks peculiar to a type of Englishwoman. But he thought of her with deep and tender love, always afraid that the world would deal with her too harshly. She had been briefly employed as a book-keeper at a well-known Swiss resort hotel – the family had celebrated her as the one with the gift for figures, along with Father, but he had since observed that it was quite ordinary. She was absurdly conscientious, the kind who would always be taken in by cruel people, whom she inevitably attracted. Poor dear Ivy.

Outside the phone booth he took a few steps then halted, stood immobile, realizing that there had been something about the call . . . something odd. He groped back over her words, the inflexions of her voice . . . remembered the whistling of the tea-kettle. Yes? Wait . . . something about that . . . why should that be unusual? He couldn't see . . . walked on. Abruptly he halted again, seeming to grasp it. The whistle had cut off while they had still been talking . . . Yes . . . It still did not quite register. Then he saw. *You could not reach the gas stove from the telephone.* The abdominal thud occurred. Somebody had turned the gas off . . . somebody else had been there. Not Mrs Tickner. Somebody in the house with her – whose presence she had concealed! He went up to his bedroom, greatly alarmed.

Mrs Tickner's cat jumping up so suddenly like that on the windowsill outside made her miss the first words of the announcement ' . . . by Albert Ketelby.' She could never remember which was 'In a Monastery Market' and which 'In a Persian Garden.' It didn't matter, they were both so nice; 'so spiffing', as Leo would say. 'That brings us to the end of this programme of . . . ' She turned the set off, adjusted her hearing aid which was crackling badly.

The reflection of the snow outside bathed the kitchen with its pale light – the blue-and-white checked table-cloth, the matching flounces on the dresser, the veined wood of the upright chairs, the brownish reproduction of *The Old Troubadour* by Miss Clara Adamson. She perched tentatively on the edge of a chair, hands in her lap; it was no good, she couldn't suppress her nervousness about Boudie's homecoming this time, because of Leo. At the same time, she knew it was ridiculous; he couldn't possibly find out, not possibly, they had been so careful.

Leo had repeated his invitation to the theatre, even pressed her; if they were lucky they could get seats for Edmund Gwenn in the revival of Galsworthy's *The Skin Game* which would make a truly memorable evening. And with both Boudie and Mrs Tickner away, she had been greatly tempted; gazing at Leo, she had told him she would love to go but . . . but . . . when next day he said he was actually going to get the tickets, she had had to ask him to defer it, to be patient. She sighed; her life was cloistered because of Boudie. But what would he do if he telephoned one eveing and she wasn't there? What would he *do*? Her pledge to Mother was sacred . . . Mother's freckled hand lifting tremblingly . . . always, Mother, always . . . old red eyebrim wet, dried skin of lower lip . . . nobody, ever . . . no, nobody . . . don't fret Mother . . . He knows I . . . yes, yes . . . he trusts me . . . never . . . never . . . now do try to rest . . .

It was all her imagination, Boudie couldn't know anything. Now she must get on. She rose resolutely and from the front room looked out; the thin snow, only patches now, sparkled frostily but the pavement looked perfectly negotiable; she would go as far as Attersole's and get two nice lamb chops for supper. Lifting her arms to put her hat on she danced with Leo, his limp quite gone, circling the floor of the divine exclusive smart aristocratically-frequented Society Club (his white tie gleaming, tailcoats flying), leaning far back against his hand, her swirling skirt brushing the table of the Hon. Evelyn and the Hon. Lady Lettice who with gracious inclinations of the head admired her and broke into spontaneous, oh irrepressible applause as they completed their final triumphant figure and stood panting and laughing and amazed at their own grace.

She slammed the front door behind her and sniffed the air of De Vere Gardens. Vibrations of excitement were making her shiver.

Sir Bertram Pendleton arrived back just after five. Ivy turned off Albert Sandler and his Palm Court Orchestra playing Selections from *Rose-Marie* and with a peculiar glance gave him a kiss. He stooped, rubbing his hands in front of the fire; the painted tin reflected the imitation glow but you couldn't pretend the warmth was adequate. Tea? No, he'd rather have a hot bath. 'I'll turn one on for you,' she said. 'The geyser's giving trouble again but . . . ' Standing, he examined his mail, quickly scanned a letter from the Medico-Legal Society . . . a debate on the death penalty, his distinguished presence greatly desirable, though they knew his firm position in favour – and as Ivy came back, turned to the door.

'It won't be ready yet, dear.'

'I have one or two things to see to first.' Hastening up the chilly stairs he pulled the door of the draughty, now faintly steamy, bathroom shut, entered his bedroom and locked the door; bed . . . the scattering of things on the chest of drawers, clothes-stand, bookshelf . . . bedside table, lamp, Roddy . . . he stood looking slowly round. It was barely noticeable but he had the impression that some of the things had been disturbed . . . the book *Miss Primrose's Teddy Tales* had been taken out and put back . . . his little Venetian glass bottle had been moved. Roddy . . . he felt a sickening thud in his chest. Some-body had examined Roddy Rockinghorse – the reins were hooked over one ear, a thing he would never do, and when he touched the horse's flank, Roddy made a tiny gliding move-ment on his runners, coming back to rest. The liquid eye, beautifully fringed with lashes, looked reproachful, on the point of tears. He dropped to his knees, examining the base and saw that it had shifted an inch or two from its normal position. They had been riding Roddy!

In one frantic stride he was at the bedside, snatched up Teddy. Oh why, why had he left Teddy behind this time? Teddy's little arms were held straight out as if he were fright-ened, were begging for comfort and protection. Pendleton kissed the nose, the fur long since worn away, hugged Teddy to his chest, rocking to and fro, then held him up at eye level. The dear little brown arm, the right one, looked looser . . . distinctly . . . the glenoid cavity . . . round the margin the glenoid labrum was distinctly worn . . . poor little dear. Who had been handling him?

The chest of drawers! flip open the lid of the shagreen-covered box; the false teeth and gums rested on the wad of cotton wool . . . the second drawer . . . the tutu . . . the folds didn't look quite right . . . Sir Bertram Pendleton realized he

64

was shaking; he saw everything threatened, the family exposed . . . everything gone . . . A wail from downstairs made him jump, then it became Ivy's warbling voice. 'Boo-uu-die! . . . Do you need anything?' He made a great effort over himself, his face in the wardrobe glass as he turned, an ugly slack mouth. He called out an answer, made his way into the bathroom, stood with his back against the locked door.

Ivy was in her usual chair by the fire knitting when he came down. 'Trying to snow again, did you see?' She glanced up at him. 'You've been doing too much again, you look tired, dear.'

'H'm . . .' He was in control of himself again. 'At all events, you've been having a quiet time.'

'Yes. Especially with Mrs Tickner away,' she said.

'What's this latest?' He picked up the book beside her. 'Clemence Dane, not your usual taste. Rather highbrow, h'm?'

'It's supposed to be spiff – awfully good.'

He sat going through the rest of his letters; there was only the click of her needles, the rustle of the paper, the faint tinny squeak of the turning 'flame' of the fire.

'What's this?' he said, after a moment. 'The Bell Off-Licence? A dozen ex of . . . what is it? . . . Em . . . of Emu?'

'Oh that, yes. I wondered, why did you buy them all at once?'

He raised his eyes to her. 'There's some mistake. They don't know me from Adam. How the devil did they get this address?'

'You must have given it to them, I suppose. It was delivered, by van, the off-licence van. The van was at the door, I don't know what Mrs Tickner or the neighbours thought.'

'Delivered? But I've only been in there once.'

Ivy smiled indulgently, put her head to one side. 'Dear Boudie . . . we've had the wine, my dear, haven't you noticed? I must say I don't mind it. Perhaps you thought it was the same bottle – or whatever they call it, some fancy name, a flagon.'

Pendleton's gaze faltered; this time an inner chill checked the spontaneous rush of his feelings, the surge of love for her was slower to reach him, so that it took him an effort before he could say 'Yes, my dear . . . foolish of me.'

'Please don't do it again, Boudie.'

Pendleton looked down at his plate, the corners of his mouth turned down, his chin quivered.

'Now don't . . . oh, never mind. You really ought to go and take them back but . . . ' She reached across the table and patted his hand. 'It's all right, don't worry. I'll go and pay the bill, though I must say I hope nobody sees me, sees me going in there. Think what Father would say! An off-licence! Anyway, there's plenty left and I dare say you'll drink it in due course.'

In the night, in spite of his fatigue, he lay awake, tormented by the thought of a stranger intruding into this secret part of his life and by the episode of the wine, a recurrence of the old pattern. Not again! There were things he did not recall . . . the young man in the off-licence, a vague oval face, a blue bow tie. What else was missing from his memory? On the ceiling a silver trapezoid slid slowly towards the wardrobe. He held himself tightly tucked up in the bedclothes, feeling as if he were buried deep in the whitish-green of an ice cavern.

Teddy's eyes were wide open and staring in the reflected moonlight.

He had no difficulty in discovering who it was, the accelerated frequency of her book-changing was a sufficient signal. With lifted chin, her back *aware*, she was loitering in Fiction A to E when an arm appeared attached to a faint smell of pipe tobacco, St Julian was the name, and put a book back. A glance, her over-eager smile, her finger, concealed, touching her hearing aid. *Have you tried this? Eoh . . . Asmetof fect A heven't neo. Oh spiffing . . .*

After a while, he was manfully, sensitively shy of her questions about himself, his domestic life, his touching little manias but finally confessed that he did his own ironing and darning sort of thing, wasn't much of a dab hand, well, you know, a cook and so forth sort of thing, so that her heart went out to and/or bled for him to the music of Giacomo Puccini and Leo Delibes (*La Valse des Fleurs*, which she privately adopted as his 'signature tune').

Concealed behind an umbrella, he watched them coming out of Pamela Purdue's Tea Caddy, the man a receding chin, reddish, fleshy wet lips, glasses, an orthopaedic boot. He had been born in Hull whence his father, a well-known wholesale fishmonger, had emigrated to Australia after a conviction for fraud; his mother had gone to live with a newsvendor and tobacconist in Cardiff. He was an orphan, had been brought up by an aunt, he had hoped to train as a chiropodist but the aunt had become absorbed with increasing passion in pursuing a couple whom she said had robbed her of a nursing-home in Skegness (about which she had collected massive documentary proof including sympathetic letters from the Poet Laureate, the Lord Chancellor and Mr Ivor Novello, all of whom supported her claim against HM Government) and neglected the young man. He was the son of an East Kent chicken farmer who had died as the result of being picked up by a horse with its teeth and shaken, and had discovered at the age of nineteen that the world is thronged with women eager to become nursemaids to men who are infantile, fumblers, engagingly 'helpless', self-absorbed and have an assumed difficulty in pronouncing the letter 'r'. At one time he had been Assistant Purser on a P & O liner running between Tilbury and Bombay, dressed up in a short white jacket known as a bum-freezer, and had kept an eye out for susceptible women passengers with whom he could, in the occupational terminology, 'poodlefake'.

The soft-voiced insidious way he had leaned towards her at the tea-table, almost touching her hand, whispering to her, then leaned back and smiled wetly at the effect of his words. Ivy kept primly a foot away from him as they walked slowly down the pavement past the shops. He had to let them get well ahead of him since Ferndale Road, then Mornington Drive, both such distinguished quiet streets, were empty. But . . . but . . . ? They were making for the golf links! Surely she . . . ? And in this weather? Ah, she had stopped, they stood briefly talking, then separated, he went on and Ivy turned back. Quick concealment; then he saw that the house had a back door in the board fence separating it from the road and golf links, probably giving on to the garden. The man glanced back

67

but Ivy was no longer in sight, then simply worked the latch, went in and shut the door. A dab of green paint on the door identified it.

From the bench where he sat watching, sheltered and partly concealed by an oak, he had a view of the rough grassy ground separating the edge of the golf links from the road and the receding line of garden fences. Directly in front of him, to the right, was a hawthorn bush, further low bushes grew beyond. Scraps of paper and tins were strewn on the ground; the light snow had not persisted.

The continuous line of fences, each with back door, was about eight feet high and hid the back gardens and the houses behind. About a third of the way along, on the fence side, was a pillar-box and, just beyond, a curving metal lamp standard; the lamp standard, seen from his bed, was this side of the pillar-box. Each section of fence varied from the rest; the first (brown paint) had a tarred patch nailed on half-way up. Through a crack in the second (ochre, grey door) a sprig of shrubbery poked out.

The man's foot swung outward at the instant of levitation and, flexing his knee slightly, he lurched, hauling the weight after him. A strand of barbed peroneal nerve ran along the top of the third section of fence (flaky blue, light-blue door). The fourth had a broad double door (dark brown); the fifth section (grey) was surmounted by a green trellis with transversely directed thickenings of the deep fascia holding the tendons in place; the door (also grey) had a dab of green paint; this was where the man lived.

Ivy and the man walked to the second fence, Ivy on the right, separate from him, paused briefly talking, then Ivy turned and went back.

The golf links extended to his right in a downward slope; he could make out a bunker and a green but these were well away down the slope; the road was protected by the rough rising ground and clumps of bushes. One clump was almost opposite the green-daubed door. Inward from this, towards the road, also opposite the door, he could see the wreck of an old perambulator.

The man, limping with the left leg, balanced his weight on the right side by a brown attaché-case. He disappeared behind the pillarbox and returned wearing a postman's helmet with postbag slung over his shoulder and limped with the other foot.

In bed he recognized the postman limping but on the bench he could not imagine a limping postman. The man walked with a rolled umbrella instead of a suitcase; he did not lean on the umbrella except twice when he turned round to look back along the road after him. People rarely came down the road, few golfers appeared. The third door (light blue) opened and let out a black and white dog, the owner remaining invisible. A light came on in a first-floor window of the house visible above the fence.

The latch on the fence door would not yield; locked. When he pressed on the thumbpiece it snapped down and the door yielded to his gentle push. The garden inside consisted of two weedy untended beds kept from spilling out on to the central pathway by short unmatched lengths of planking stuck edge-ways into the earth. He peered in through the glass panel of the back door, turned the knob.

Inside the kitchen, painted chocolate, there was a white ugly sink, draining-board, gas stove with brown-stained saucepan, table covered with oil-cloth in a china-blue and white geometric pattern. A short passage directly opposite the back door led through past a dark sitting-room to the front room and entrance; hall-stand and stairs up to the left. Sounds from above.

There was a region in his head that was the house through which he was climbing, papered with green varnished wallpaper and when the man appeared naked at the head of the stairs with his scribbles of hair wet, he was hardly surprised; but inexplicably this image overlapped with the face of the young man in the Bell Off-Licence, twisting his bow tie and offering a flagon of Emu, and for a moment he could not tell which it was, the young man or the Librarian who lay with mouth open on the bathroom floor. Jammed into the corner of the landing was a tall stand meant for a plant with a bulbous empty brass pot on it, and above, a picture of a golden-haired boy gazing heavenward with the legend *Bubbles*. The bathroom door, half open, disclosed linoleum in a pattern of green and red squares, a section of bath, an overturned cork-topped stool, the bare feet.

The sound of the water filling the bath, which had covered his approach, ceased as the taps were turned off. Pressing into the corner of the landing, he rapidly shed his overcoat (long apron underneath) and pulled on his surgical gloves. The weapon had to be heavy to produce a sufficient blow (kinetic energy equals mass multiplied by the square of velocity divided by two). He heard small indefinite sounds as the man moved about inside the bathroom; the tap dripped. The door open silently on the man's back. Shearing wound on skull; mechanically he reached out, slopped water from the bath on to the floor and the feet, as if he had already foreseen the circumstances. The cadaver lay on its side, mouth gaping. Whereupon an image immediately arose of himself preceding Skinner and Co up the stairs, removing the brass pot from the stand and replacing it with his bag, methodically folding his overcoat over the landing banisters and, putting on apron and gloves, entering.

At the bottom of the stairs he heard the man humming *La Valse des Fleurs* and swirling the water heavily in the bath. It was necessary to wait until these sounds were replaced by the gurgle of the bath water running away. Ready in apron and gloves he was about to start up when the man flung the bathroom door open, limped heavily and wetly out, took up something out of sight from the landing and returned to the bathroom leaving the door open. Softly up the stairs, close to the wall. *His glasses*; they were either steamed over or he was not wearing them. Nevertheless the man's startled open-mouthed look at the last minute, too late of course. He stooped . . .

At the back door in the fence, about to emerge, he was startled to see a couple occupying the bench under the oak, a youth with curly ginger hair and a girl, dark, bobbed and prettily plump. Looking closer he saw that they were engaged in . . . no doubt about it . . . sexual dalliance – in which the girl had the initiative! Head down, she was . . . ! His outrage boiled up, simmered but under his anxiety to leave, subsided. Occupied as they were . . . he hung back, holding the door ajar. Steps approached outside and before he could shut the door, a spaniel ran in, looked up at him, nose twitching. He made an abrupt movement, the dog lifted a paw, finally darted out. Gently he shut the door, stood facing it. The light all at once became suffused with yellow and he realized that the street-light had been switched on. The steps outside reached the door in a faint odour of shag . . . passed on; he waited until they had faded and eased the door open again. The couple had shifted position but was still there. Lowering his head, he stepped out and shut the door behind him and turning his back, walked off the other way.

He was galloping in his detachable shirtsleeves on Roddy Rockinghorse, hair tousled, flying over ditches and hedges, wheeling, pulling up short and spurring off again in a new direction. A sound outside made him rein in and pause, feeling Roddy's sides bellowing under his legs. He leaned forward, stroked Roddy's lovely yellow neck. It was nothing; a dig with his heels – on again!

The door opened and Ivy came into the room; he slowed to a canter, stretched his neck towards her, baring the false teeth and gums. Ivy crossed to the window, pulled the curtains closer together, turned round with a gentle expression.

'Have you been naughty again, Boudie?'

6

Dr Percy Redpath, settled at his usual corner table at the Two Compasses with his paper propped up in front of him and a pint of beer at hand, was not thinking about his lunch so much as congratulating himself that he had managed to elude sharing it with Dr Wilfred Carr. In these last few months he had changed ideas about young Carr. He would never have said, of course, that he found his looks very agreeable – those fly-button eyes, his short-back-and-sides reddish hair, his splay-foot walk; but he was certainly clever, even, in patches, brilliant. But his engagement to a peer's daughter had given him ambitious ideas. Decidedly too pushy, young Carr. So far had they come from the early deference, 'Yes, Dr Redpath . . . of course, sir . . . ' that Carr, now visible as a born intriguer, had started a sort of underground 'Get rid of Redpath' campaign to elbow him out of his hospital appointment, and with the noble lord's influence might even have some success (everybody had enemies) though Redpath believed he could hold the allegiance of most of the hospital committee.

Dr Redpath took a swallow of beer. Perhaps he had spoken too freely to Carr at the beginning? At all events, Carr was now puffing himself up as a potential giant killer, if you could believe this talk about Pendleton. It was true, he himself had been less than forceful giving evidence in the Sperati case; he simply had not been sure the man could have strangled the woman with those mutilated hands. Pendleton, as usual, had had no doubts whatever. It was plain to him, Pendleton had averred, as it must be obvious to the jury, that with those pitiful stumps and most of the arm muscles gone, he couldn't have exercised any pressure on the victim's throat – would hardly have been able to hold her still, and of course she would be struggling violently.

Yet after Sperati's acquittal and conviction on the lesser burglary charge, he had confessed to the murder; he had indeed strangled her, in fact, through long practice, he had a ferocious grip with his fingerstumps. Pendleton had been wrong; the jury had been over-awed by him.

Deplorable, no doubt of it, almost, as things went, inevitable. But the situation with Pendleton had not grown up overnight . . . and Carr was rushing in where it was essential to be exact, precise, prudent. All very well for him to maintain that there was 'something peculiar' about Pendleton . . . it was too loose, too vague; and to be more specific would be risky: the judiciary, the police, the Home Office had confidence in Pendleton and Dr Wilfred Carr was relatively inexperienced and unknown. In any event the profession would, as they said, 'close ranks'. Young Carr was going to find himself in an awkward position if he wasn't careful.

The whole thing promised to be enjoyable. He took another sip of beer. Nothing like seeing another fellow poke himself in the eye.

'Underdone beef, sir?'

'Thank you, Ted.'

'I'll bring you the mustard.'

He managed to dodge the request for his services from Newberry of the Warwick police but when Skinner called him in on the Ipswich trunk murder, he was obliged to go. It meant two days' absence and, on his return, another full day's work in the morgue which he finished with a cold in the head. The sporadic nervous pulsing in his abdominal aorta had recurred and he wondered if it weren't an incipient aneurism; the neck-stretching tic also annoyed him but he could not manage to throw it off.

Nothing had come out. Ivy, her usual self on the phone, had not referred to it; they did not take the local newspaper. Impossible to insert himself into the case without being called in. In most of the Metropolitan districts he could simply call at the coroner's office and at the least expect to pick up a hint. But the coroner here was Dysart . . . and he could see Dysart's hard-mouthed pleated face turned to him, his eyes screwed up with surprise and suspicion if he 'dropped in'. Dysart was pugnacious, an awkward customer; they had inevitably run across each other many times; until lately, Dysart had been in the habit of turning up at the scene of a crime, if it happened to be in one of his large Metropolitan districts, soon after Pendleton himself had got there with the police. But Dysart had formed his own panel of pathologists (including Redpath) and, when he could, gave them the work.

And there was the other thing . . . common professional knowledge: Dysart was on bad terms with his local doctors. They had petitioned him, protesting that he consistently refused to take them into account when it came to inquests or post-mortems. Dysart had brushed them aside. In several cases, on the strength of complaints or 'suspicions' by relatives, usually ill-founded, he had disregarded the death certificate signed by the patient's own doctor and ordered a post-mortem. And when the pathologist had found – as quite often happened – that the patient had not died of whatever the doctor had certified but of something else, the local practitioner was even more offended.

Yet some action was necessary.

On the third morning after his return he walked round to the coroner's court, a slate-roofed building in Wesleyan gothic crouching in dusty shrubbery. At the far end of the empty court-room by the coroner's chair, he pulled open the door to Dysart's office; but instead of Dysart's doggy face at the desk, the watery eye of old Becherwaise looked up through his glasses. The old man rose to his feet, chin a bit wobbly. 'Well . . . Sir Bertram – this is a – to what do we owe this honour? Quite like old . . . Ah, you know – ? No, of course you don't, Sergeant Cooch wasn't here.' He introduced Pendleton and the sergeant, obviously impressed, nodded, 'Yes, sir, of course.' Becherwaise had been coroner for years before retiring at the time of the borough reorganization.

It appeared that Dysart was away and Becherwaise was deputizing for him. Declining a seat, saying this was simply a casual call, Sir Bertram Pendleton explained that he was writing up his cases and seemed to have lost the card about the Leitch strangling. 'Unusually interesting case. Dysart will remember it. I wonder if he'd mind passing on his file. Refresh my memory.'

Naturally, glad to; Sergeant Cooch would get it for him straight away. Wait; Sir Bertram held up a hand. 'Dysart's rather touchy on these things. I'd prefer to have his authorization. I'll come by again when he's back.'

Certainly, certainly. Becherwaise would make a note. Well . . . well . . . they chatted, Sir Bertram Pendleton allowed himself to yield to Becherwaise's insistence that he take a seat, for just a moment. Becherwaise was visibly relieved when Sergeant Cooch excused himself and went out. Becherwaise seemed to be debating something in his mind.

'Well, I must go.' Pendleton rose at length.

'Well, yes – ah – Sir Bertram . . . ' the old man laid a detaining hand on his sleeve. 'I wonder . . . if it's not . . . I wonder if I might ask you a great service. I know how busy you are . . . but it would be of great help . . . inestimable help. You could do me a great . . . a great favour.'

Pendleton frowned, looking doubtful. Becherwaise's face was compressed in pain. 'I dare say you've heard of the diff-the trouble – the difficulties we've been having, I mean with the local people, local practitioners. Dysart's got up their noses. I'm not . . . mind you, I'm not saying who's right. I'm not saying who's wrong. It was just my idea . . . just trying to smooth things over, for everybody's sake . . . I mean, to get things smoother, you understand?'

In an endeavour to appease the local doctors, old Becherwaise had called in one of them, the most vocal among the protestors against Dysart, to do a post-mortem, the first time this had happened for years. Well, it had turned out to be a mistake; the man had not had enough experience (Dysart had been right there), he had made a mess and the result was inconclusive. To call in one of Dysart's panel of pathologists for a second autopsy would create a fresh row on both sides and Dysart on his return would be furious.

Pendleton said, 'I sympathize but I don't see – '

'I don't like to – but if you would undertake it, Sir Bertram . . . With your authority . . . certainly help me . . . help us all here. I mean, they'd have to accept it.

'What, do another PM?'

'Yes.'

Pendleton declined, made heavy weather of it, dragged in ethics; Becherwaise, glimpsing salvation, pleaded, insisted. 'You would settle it. I'm sure you – '

'Bit of a hornet's nest, isn't it?'

'Oh, your presence would stop all that . . . Your eminence . . . I mean, your . . . '

Pendleton considered further, shook his head, finally after more hesitation said, 'You'd have to ask me officially.'

'Of course. Ask you officially. Of course.'

'What is the case?'

'You probably saw something about it in the *Independent*. Small paragraph.'

'I never read the *Independent*.'

'Woman named Jessop, dead in her kitchen.'

The four knitting needles got mixed up, she missed the stitch, dropped it, dropped another, jerked at the wool and the ball fell and rolled across the floor. Really! Ivy laid the knitting aside. With an effort over herself she smoothed her skirt, adjusted the hairpins in her earphones, reached for a Player's No 3, decided no, she didn't want it. Poor Boudie, he didn't realize the strain it always produced for her. Yet this was the moment when she must stand by him with all her strength, when he needed her protection most, when her pledge to Mother must be fulfilled to the last. Of course he knew she knew . . . he knew . . . but utter silence, the watchful formality of their manner with each other was the rule. This time she had concealed her friendship with the man . . . but it hadn't helped. In a strange way he already seemed someone she had hardly . . . Leo . . . yes.

It was no good, she couldn't sit still. She rose and turned on the wireless, somebody singing 'Onaway, Awake, beloved!', usually one of her favourites but this morning it made her hearing aid buzz horribly and she turned it off again. Her fingers drummed on the cabinet, she fetched a duster from the kitchen and passed unseeing round the room flicking the duster at furniture and objects, pausing occasionally as the same mystifying questions repeated themselves in her mind. Why Leo's pipe? Why had Boudie put it in his apron pocket? What was the meaning of it? She was sure she hadn't made a mistake. It had been there before she had put the apron in the dirty linen; now the pipe was nowhere to be seen. Coming across it she had thought for a moment that Boudie had taken up – then recognized the little silver band round the stem. It was Leo's.

And the cat? He had terrified it in some way. What was the meaning of that?

Before she had finished, she heard the tap at the back door and Mrs Tickner's voice. In the kitchen, Mrs Tickner was stooping and peering under the sink. 'Oh,' she straightened up. 'I knew you used to leave a saucer there for him. Has he been in?'

'I haven't seen him.' It was almost as if Mrs Tickner was accusing her of having enticed her cat away. Mrs Tickner stood blankly staring into space. 'What did I come for? Timmy, yes – but something else. Oh yes, my keys – there they are.' Ivy thought she had actually been using some sort of reddish-gingerish make-up pencil on her eyebrows, she could see the half-inch extra at the ends, a slightly lighter colour than the rest; a woman of her age, it was dreadful. Mrs Tickner turned her sharp eyes directly on her. 'You know, it's a most peculiar thing. Most peculiar thing. Do you know what I think? I think somebody has deliberately frightened the poor thing, Timmy, I mean. Frightened the life out of him.' She tightened her mouth, gave a cock to her head and paused to let the effect sink in. 'Deliberately.'

Ivy felt awful; for one wild second the vision flashed before her as she threw herself on Mrs Tickner's compassion, clasped her knees, confessed to her it had been Boudie, begged, implored her to understand . . . but the thought of Mrs Tickner's

78

triumph, her ghastly smile of 'I knew it all along' wiped it out. Absolutely impossible.

'Why would anyone do such a thing?'

'I put some liver out,' Mrs Tickner said. 'He's never refused liver. I went to Munro's, I got a little bit of fish, his favourite fish and put it out. He won't come near it. And I think I saw him! When I opened the back door yesterday morning, just a flash, but he flew off. Somebody's been cruel to him. I know it. He's been frightened to death.'

Mrs Tickner's eyes were fixed on her intently. Ivy said, 'You're imagining things . . . Let's . . . would you like a cup of tea?'

Mrs Tickner looked as if Ivy had made the offer to mollify her, and declined. Her manner said she was in command here. Her expression changed slightly, she began to talk of a visit she had made to the new Ladies' Department they had opened at Guthrie's and the interesting lines they were carrying, edging into the room as she talked. Ivy felt weakly foolish for not being able to get rid of her. In the end, Mrs Tickner picked up the library book on the table. 'Oh, the Warwick Deeping . . . the same? Yes, I thought it might be a new one.' She flipped open the cover. 'You've had this out – good heavens, you've got a fine, you know that? Look, it's well overdue.'

'Yes, I forgot to take it back.'

'You've been getting a lot of new books out lately, that's why I thought . . .'

Ivy lit a Player's No 3. 'Well, excuse me. I've got a phone call to make.'

Mrs Tickner gave a last glance round and through the open door beyond. 'Don't forget if you see Timmy, even if it's late. I've put the fish out on the windowsill.'

With some reluctance, yet generously unsparing of his time as ever, Sir Bertram Pendleton, having done the post mortem on Mrs Jessop (a chronic alcoholic; cause of death rhabdomyolysis) agreed to the pressing request of Detective-Inspector Kilburn of the local police to look at another body, that of Leopold Cox, the borough librarian.

'You'll pardon the liberty, Sir Bertram, but you being here it's a golden opportunity. That's why I came over as soon as Sergeant Cooch told me. Body's right here, won't take you long. Our man, that's Dr Griffin, put it down to an accident but I'm not satisfied. Something fishy there.'

'I want to hear what the police have to say,' Dysart said; Sergeant Cooch bent over and gave him the name. 'Yes, Detective Inspector Kilburn.'

Dysart, returned to duty, was conducting the inquest in his usual brisk way. At the table below the bench where Dysart sat under the royal coat of arms, Sir Bertram Pendleton waited with folded hands to be called. Dysart hadn't looked particularly glad to see him when he had handed in his report the day before. A dozen people, mostly women, were dispersed through the public seats, the sound of heavy rain and the gurgling of gutters came from outside and the mixed smell of earth, shrubbery and wet clothes permeated the court. All at once, while Kilburn was being sworn, Dysart stood up. 'What are you doing with that cigarette?' Whereupon all heads turned in unison; Dysart was bristling at an elderly man at the back. 'Yes, you! Put it out at once! Where do you think you are, at a football match? This is the King's court. Be bringing bottles of beer here next. And put that paper away.'

'Bus map, your honour.'

'I don't care what it is. I'll have proper respect shown here. Now, Inspector, if you please . . . '

Kilburn, a good looking fair-haired man of about forty-five, with a quiet manner, gave the routine evidence of being called to the house, the body, the police surgeon's examination, police inquiries about the deceased. Sir Bertram Pendleton, sitting filling in official forms for two of the day's post-mortems, as he usually did in court, eased his neck in his collar.

'We've heard Dr Griffin say he thinks it was an accident, the classic slip on the wet bathroom floor. What makes you think otherwise?'

'With respect, sir, I'm not saying it was otherwise.' The Inspector's fluffy moustache made a little movement. 'But we

80

have certain suspicions; there may have been an intruder. We found traces of earth from the garden in the kitchen and the hall. Faint traces. We made an appeal for witnesses, anybody who might have seen such an intruder entering the house; one gentleman, Captain Hope-Messenger, a neighbour, informed us that he was walking his dog along Orpington Drive, that's the road that runs behind the houses. He had the impression that his dog actually darted into the back garden of one of the houses, it may have been number 32, he's not sure, he rather thinks it was 40, and ran out again; but when he passed the back door it was shut. Captain Hope-Messenger is here, if you wish to hear him, sir.'

'He only had an impression, he didn't in fact see anything?'

'No, sir.'

'We're not impressed by impressions, Inspector.'

An uncertain obsequious titter from the court.

'Anything else?'

'Yes, sir. In the kitchen waste-bin we found a scrap of paper with a few words on it. Seemed to be a half-burnt note. We managed to decipher it. As near as we can make out, there's the 't' of a previous word, then the words 'tell Bondi' or 'Bodi'. We think this is an Italian or an Australian name. We are making inquiries along these lines for an Italian or an Australian subject who might have known Mr Cox . . . so far without success.'

'Any known enemies? Any . . . um . . . unusual habits?'

'No, sir.'

'These traces of earth; the deceased might have brought them in himself?'

'Well, we can't exclude it, sir.'

Dysart made a note. 'As I understand it, nothing was stolen from the house?'

'No, sir.'

'Nothing disturbed to suggest your hypothetical intruder?'

'No. There was one other thing, sir. We found a small deposit of half-burnt tobacco on the bathroom floor; the deceased smoked a pipe, we found his tobacco pouch but only one new pipe, hardly been smoked.'

'H'm.' This didn't seem to strike Dysart very forcibly. He

finished writing, straightened up in the chair. 'I have had a report from Sir Bertram Pendleton who was asked to examine the body. This was done in my absence and I suppose I must accept it, though I can't see why it was necessary to go outside the normal well-established practice of this court. We have perfectly qualified men here to do such work and a devoted body of medical practitioners always ready to serve in the public interest. Sir Bertram Pendleton, please.'

Eh? Oh yes. Pendleton slipped the forms into his bag, walked to the witness stand and, having taken the oath, began to read his full report. 'On 8 April I examined the body of . . . '

Dysart cut in. 'Not necessary to go through the whole thing again. Hand it up. What was the cause of death, in your opinion? In plain language, please.'

'Severe damage to the right side of the brain due to the head striking a hard object, such as the side of the bath, in a fall. I found a torn scalp wound three inches long, severe membrane tears on the brain itself, haemorrhage and deep contusions, that is on the right-hand side, marked *contre-coup* effect on the other side.'

'In other words, a fractured skull. I want terms the jury can understand.'

'In this case there was no fracture. In my experience only about two out of three fatal cranial injuries show fractures of the skull.'

'What was that foreign word you used?'

'*Contre-coup.*'

'Kindly expain that to the jury.'

'Yes. It means counter-blow. *Contre-coup* is a type of brain injury found exactly opposite the site of impact. This is be-cause, under the impact, the brain as a whole moves inside the skull – piles up, if you like, on the other side. The pial vessels and arachnoid tetherings are stretched. The whole brain is often injured.'

'That is what happened in this case?'

'Yes. The deceased was otherwise healthy, apart from a congenitally deformed foot.'

'He was lame, in other words. And could the lameness have contributed to his losing his balance?'

'Certainly. He would not have the ability of a normal person to recover.'

'But you could rule out foul play?'

'Oh yes. In my view it was a commonplace accident.'

'Thank you, Sir Bertram.'

Dysart looked down at his papers, shuffled them, wrote something. People coughed, the rumble of a heavy horse and cart went by outside. Finally, Dysart looked up again. 'I hesitate to impose a deferment in this case. Without the police bringing forward something much more definite it would not be justified. In view of the evidence, which has not been contested in any quarter, I shall direct the jury to bring in a verdict of accidental death.'

Outside the court, Pendleton caught sight of a half-familiar face among the people going away . . . Mrs Tickner? A huddle of umbrellas got in the way before he could get a proper view, he could not be sure – he jumped back from a lorry bouncing past, spraying him with puddle – and collided with Inspector Kilburn. 'Oh – sorry, Inspector . . . Well, that's settled, anyway.'

Kilburn gave him a quizzical look. 'I'm not so sure, sir. Something funny about it.' He ducked to the police car pulling up. 'Give you a lift, Sir Bertram?'

'No thanks, I'll walk.'

'Eh? . . . In this . . . ?' The Inspector looked up; but Sir Bertram Pendleton had gone.

A little *entrechat* . . . an elaborate reverence . . . The fluffy tutu fresh back from the laundry ('for my niece,' Ivy always said. 'Such a big girl, but so graceful.') bounced deliciously on his hips; tonight he was also wearing the red tights. Through the doors to the dining-room he could hear Ivy talking to Mrs Tickner . . . Harpy orchestral undulations for the dying swan . . . Oops! too near the fireplace . . . every time he thumped on the floor the conversation next door ceased, then Ivy hastily filled the breach. They only had to open the door and there he was! He loved wearing the tutu downstairs; he was going to have dinner in it tonight . . . Oh come in, Detective Chief-

Inspector . . . a dismemberment? Why certainly . . . you don't mind me coming just like this, a little informality is sometimes helpful . . . oh, wait, my teeth! All you have is a saucerful of extra-peritoneal fat? Why my dear sir, I can tell you age, height, hair colour, education, birthplace, personal idiosyncrasies and cultural affinities from that . . . certainly . . . without question.

Silence next door. A *saut de biche* . . . a *déboulé* . . . another reverence . . . The sound of the back door shutting; a moment later Ivy, shutting the door behind her.

'Boudie, dear, you mustn't, you really mustn't come down like that. Mrs Tickner was here . . . just here, in the dining-room . . . I'm sure she thought it was strange I didn't bring her in here . . . I'm sure she heard you.'

'I was dancing *The Dying Emu* . . . *Emulake Ballet.*'

'Please, Boudie, no more now.'

'I want to have dinner like this.'

'Oh dear. Wait . . . wait there, let me pull the kitchen curtains before you come through.'

As usual in mid-afternoon, the Library was empty. Ivy lingered a moment in the Ws (. . . Waddell . . . h'mm . . . Weyman, Stanley . . . Wells, H. G. *Mr Blettsworthy on* . . . no, nobody called Blettsworthy . . . Woolf . . . Oh neo, definitely not . . .) aware out of the corner of her eye of the man still studying a book a little farther along, something back in the Rs. She had an instinctive feeling that he wasn't a reader, had not come for a book, and oddly his appearance seemed to be vaguely familiar – the moustache, the weathered look of his face, his stiff-backed bearing (she loved his hands but why wasn't he wearing a hat?). Forty, forty-two; fair hair severely trimmed back and sides, not exactly distinguished but handsome. Military? She saw him on his horse, a black mare with white flecks of foam, leading the review with the regimental colours.

She passed on, round the end of the stack and resumed her search for something nice . . . Mason . . . Mottram . . . no . . . Maugham . . . Macaulay . . . through the Ls . . . he reappeared round the end of the stack, apparently entirely absorbed in his search, sometimes bending to the books lower down, now and then reaching up to take one out . . . but in fact interested in *her*. He was following her, trying to summon the courage to speak to her . . . always so easy here: 'Splendid book. Have you read it?' or 'Excuse me (or 'Pardon' he'd say) I wonder if you could help me choose something for my aunt (never wife, of course)? She's poorly and I'm rather at a loss. Something light, I hope you don't mind my asking?' That was why some men came here. Come to think of it, she had seen him hanging round the Library before – *that* was it, she had definitely seen him here before. Yet he did not look the dubious type. Gazing at something by Susan Glaspell, she couldn't help smiling; their little flight and pursuit round the bookstacks, first one, then the other, never a word, had become rather entertaining.

Abruptly, turning girlishly on her heel to make her skirt swing, she turned away to Biography and Memoirs . . . *Thirty Years with Horn and Hound . . . Lord Curzon . . . By Nile and Tigris*. He was still in Fiction, his back turned, but when she moved on to History she saw him step across too and begin slowly to edge along towards her. Twice he looked up from the book he was holding and seemed to glance over towards the small room beyond, now empty, where they kept the Children's Books.

As if struck by a sudden thought, she returned to the beginning of Biography, which entailed passing behind him, extracted a book at random and stood looking over the top of it towards the frosted glass panels of Leo's old office. The door was ajar but all she could see inside was the edge of the calendar and the corner of the green metal filing cabinet. Leo's desk was out of sight, she had not yet managed to catch a glimpse of his successor, but as she watched a shadow moved behind the glass, the vague shape of a head and shoulders, from which, because of some arrangement of the electric light in the office, emerged a second head, clearer and more solid-looking, as if (the reverse of what might be expected) a body had emerged from a ghost; yet the voice she heard at the same moment was indistinct and wavy. An uncomfortable feeling enveloped her, she returned the book to the shelf and saw that the man with the moustache had left History and was rapidly approaching her.

She moved away to the two rows of newly returned books racked by the small open staff enclosure at the entrance where the woman library assistant sat occupied with some paper-work. A moment later, the man followed suit. Now he was giong to say something . . . rather unfortunate he had chosen this spot. Nevertheless, her discomfort yielded to a pleasant tingle of excitement, negligently she slipped a hand under her scarf and turned up her hearing aid. He was six feet away . . . edging along, turned his head towards her.

'Oh . . . er, Mr – Inspector . . . ' The woman assistant was looking up. 'I've got what you – ' Instantly he strode into the enclosure, bent over the woman, speaking in an undertone.

Ivy, without a book, pressed against the wicket-gate exit which the woman, looking red-faced and embarrassed with the man still bent over her, released with her foot pedal. Without moving his downbent head, the man looked up and for an instant his grey eyes, slightly globular in this raised position, met Ivy's. She was close enough to see the tiny pleats and texture of skin, a red vein, the liquid retained by the rim of the eye in which the eyeball, moving to follow her, glided rather unpleasantly. He gave no sign, she passed on. On the steps she smiled to herself; how entertaining! The Library Inspector! Of course. What a pity he hadn't spoken to her. From the concrete pathway outside, through the windows, she saw a ginger-haired youth emerge from the Children's Books section and the Inspector, who looked somewhat red-faced now, marching up to him, neck thrust out, as if he had caught the young man in some misbehaviour.

7

The evening was so mild and pleasant that they had decided to get off the bus and walk home across the Common. A commonplace streak of cloud dramatized by a purple edge crossed the sky in the setting sun. Small darker patches of smoke-cloud sailed by, lower down, like puffs from cannon-shot.

Ivy had spoken of nothing but the performance ever since they had left the theatre, surprising him by her close acquaintance with the lives of the actors, the playwright and their Society connections; the whole thing had bored him and he had looked with horror at the audience of middle-aged and elderly women, full of chatter and enthusiasm for the mediocre play (a critical triumph, naturally). And the fact of coming out while it was still light, emerging into the day street, had added to the depressing effect. But it was the rarest of occasions, the two of them out together to a mid-week matinée, and he had pretended to enjoy it for Ivy's sake – recognizing that she had been right . . . he was dead tired from overwork, all summer without a holiday, and needed a break. And the heavy programme of examinations and lectures three times a week at the university medical school was approaching.

A loose ball from a cricket match scooted past, pursued by a dog. A fat red-faced woman chased a boy in a red shirt, much too agile for her. A young man in steel-rimmed glasses was trying unsuccessfully to launch a box kite.

He wordlessly squeezed Ivy's hand holding his arm and smiled, glad that the outing had been a success for her. She had been rather fearful of going but her new hearing aid had evidently worked well and she was so happy . . . dear, sweet girl. One jarring moment, a youngish man in the theatre had seemed to know her . . . but perhaps he had been mistaken. And one of the actors, fortunately in a minor role, had reminded him unpleasantly of RM, the hawk-nosed Scot who had consorted with Ivy all those years ago . . . had tried to seduce her. The thought still gave him a flush of anger – the man's sedulousness, his egotistical lack of sensibility, combined even with a dash of condescension! Fortunately he had gone off on his own account . . . not without some effort to take her with him as his mistress.

He was annoyed at himself for letting it all come up and disturb him today, and patted her hand again. The walk across the Common was pleasant. They discussed the acquisition of a radiogram, an expensive, not to say luxurious item which Ivy thought would not only add to their prestige – one of the long shiny models would look so well in the drawing-room – but actually provide enjoyment. Of course they would have to buy gramophone records but they could be guided to some extent by Christopher Stone whose programmes on the Home Service Ivy listened to regularly.

As they approached the far edge of the Common, the mingled sounds and shouts of the open air were infused with the music of a fairground. He spotted the site ahead, called her attention to it with a jerk of his arm and chin, and she nodded delightedly. The fair had evidently reached the end of its stay, the men were dismantling the stands among a lot of strewn paper and bottles, but the last roundabout was still working. They paused, watching it come to a halt and the children and adults get down.

Sir Bertram detached himself, stepped up on to the roundabout. The pipey music was loud. Lovely ostriches, transpierced by twisted brass poles, a stodgy swan, beautiful horses. He caressed the nearest horse – yellow and blue neck, flying green and red mane, gleaming with the patina of countless loving hands, a little pad of red velvet for a saddle. The horse was at full stretch. Somebody among the onlookers behind called to him – Ivy, her eyes wide, was jerking her head

88

urging him to get on. 'Go on!' her open mouth soundlessly said.

A wild urge took him, simply to let go, turn and toss her his homburg hat (his 'front page hat, known to millions' she called it), to climb on to the horse and go whirling round cheering, his open coat blowing out behind him. He glanced round again at Ivy – for final encouragement – and saw that, head slightly turned, she was exchanging a sly sidelong look with somebody among the spectators near by . . . his eye sought – the man he had noticed at the theatre. So he had not been mistaken! The man was thirty-fiveish, good-looking in a saturnine way with long jaw, cleft chin, carefully done hair, a shirt with a broad blue stripe, suede shoes. An appropriate name came to him from nowhere, Jasper Kenderdine.

Quickly he faced back to the horse; perhaps she had not noticed that he had seen . . . His calves were shaky, the nervous beating in the abdominal aorta started up. He swayed as if the roundabout had abruptly begun to whirl round perilously close in a flash of hoofs and brass.

A man smelling of beer pushed roughly up, lifted a child on to the horse and himself climbed up behind; slowly the roundabout began to turn. Sir Bertram Pendleton controlled himself, hurriedly descended and made his way back to Ivy; her smiling expression, the sideways tilt of her head said only that she was sorry he hadn't got on.

They continued to walk back arm in arm down the edge of the worn grass in the deepening evening; the landscape became bleaker, they passed tall menacing clumps of reeds in water, ragged birds cawed desolately in the trees and the breeze began to carry a chill, and the idea of lack, of a terrible vacancy. Confused half-thoughts filled his mind, mingling with the voices of the people round about, the necessity to escape into the secrecy of his work, the weak, foolish, unattractive face of his dear sister.

The man remained obliquely somewhere behind them but when they were half-way down De Vere Gardens, a blaring exhaust overtook them and a grey round-nosed AC sports two-seater driven by Jasper Kenderdine flashed by and disappeared round the corner. The road was empty, so that his tootle on the horn had been pointless unless for her; but Ivy's expression, when he looked, was unchanged.

Superimposed on the mortuary slab where the handsome blonde young woman lay, hardly a visible sign of injury except the small lacerations on her right shoulder and right elbow, was the red-stone Victorian block of flats of Murchison Mansions off Baker Street where Jasper Kenderdine lived, whitened steps outside, a dim entrance faintly illuminated by a pair of heavily framed self-reflecting mirrors on either side, two pairs of fake-marble columns and, deeper in, a stone arch under which rose the stairs, carpeted in red, and a thick banister. The plaque of the lift-button gleamed in the dim reddish gloom. The lift (a modern addition) was enclosed in a fine wire cage, the mesh thickened by a sort of fine black fur; on the wall he noted a light-bracket with a tulip-shaped shade; but he did not press the switch.

The right eye was protruding and engorged in a particular way, and he suspected what he would find before he proceeded.

His steps fell without a sound on the turkey carpet. First floor heavy double doors in the uniform magenta red of the building and a round brass bell-push. He leaned back over the banister and craned up; a rising succession of oblong mirror-images of banister and moulded ceiling.

It was probable that the internal carotid artery having been ruptured within the cavernous sinus, an arteriovenous fistula had occurred, causing an abnormal reflux of blood from the cavernous sinus into the ophthalmic veins . . . the result, without a doubt, of a fracture at the base of the skull.

The interlocking images gave way to the vision of Ivy sitting on a man's knee, her face brushed by a man with an aquiline nose and cleft chin who instantly the door opened made a rapid movement of one hand . . .

From the ABC teashop diagonally across from the Mansions or from Angelo's Snacks the other way, he could note the comings and goings – but he had no time to sit watching! On some evenings, long after dark, he found himself in this strange new territory gazing past the waitresses and cash desk (already preparing to close) or between the twin pillars of cheese and ham sandwiches, the tarmac gleaming wetly outside in the squiggles of electric light and the red flash of buses. What did they think of him, these people, never as indifferent as they seemed . . . some old fool watching for a young woman who was tormenting him? The mansions, the steps, the entrance, the curtains of the first-floor bay window were imprinted on his mind.

The gloved hand removed the light-bulb in the entrance, withdrew into the dark zone behind the stairs. The twin lozenges of glass in the front door were faintly outlined by the street lamps outside, flushed occasionally in the headlights of a passing taxi. A black cut-out appeared against them, the door panel swung open, the cut-out advanced into the hall turning down collar, unbuttoning coat, paused to press the lift-button, in vain, and abandoning this, turned to the stairs. A startled exclamation 'Who . . . ? What the – ?' A gasp.

Two or three more women this year among the rows of students before him. He felt weary . . . Behind him the blackboard wiped clean; with care he placed the full glass on top of his desk. 'Well now, if you are all settled down . . . The first point in our introduction to Special Pathology and Medical Jurisprudence this afternoon is an eminently simple one. I have here a glass of urine; clear appearance, no crystals or cylinders, probable absence of glucose or protein, possibly a few leucocytes. I dip my finger in thus . . . can you all see? At the back there, yes? . . . and if I then taste it . . . thus (finger in mouth), I notice something . . . What is it I notice? No . . . ? Very well. Will you kindly pass the glass round, the gentleman in front here . . . take it and taste it, do as I have just done, dip in . . . yes, and pass it along to your colleagues so that they may do the same . . . That's right . . . go on . . . just so . . . that's right, pass it along . . . get a good taste . . . See if you can answer the question . . . I have another glass here, if you would take it, sir and pass it along to the right . . . that's right, dip in . . . yes, young lady, everybody has a taste . . . '

He waited till they had all finished. 'All done now? Very

well, pass the glasses forward then . . . Put them there. Well, now we have all got the taste in our mouths for the next hour, what do we conclude from this simple test? You noticed that I dipped this finger into the urine but put this one into my mouth? You did not? Then what, gentlemen, is the first thing we learn in pathology? To observe.'

It was a comfortable room, a big light-brown silk-covered sofa facing the fireplace, leather armchair on the right side, table with a green and white Chinese-style vase made into a lamp on the left. The sepia photograph of Ivy in a green-enamelled frame on the mantelpiece taken some years ago in Switzerland, was a surprise.

'Come in, sit down.' Kenderdine, evidently amused by the encounter, passed behind the sofa, gestured to the leather chair. Facing him in hat and gloves, he said 'Thank you, no.'

'What . . . ?' Kenderdine looked puzzled, yet still entertained.

'You have been seeing my sister.'

'Your sister . . . ? Oh . . . well – yes.' Kenderdine laughed.

'I must ask you to break off with her.'

'What on earth . . . ? Most astonishing thing I ever heard. Why should I?'

'Let me see that photograph of her, would you?'

'What . . . ? Photograph . . . ? Oh . . . ' he turned, reached out for the photograph.

The photograph fell, the glass smashed . . . A gloved hand picked it up, extracted the photograph.

'If a weapon is found, the first question the doctor will ask himself is: could the wound have been inflicted with that weapon? If it is a firearm, what was the range and from what direction was it fired? Unless there is some hitched-up arrangement to pull the trigger – which the doctor will find in place – a wound can only be self-inflicted from within the subject's reach, say about a metre. Anything beyond that is not necessarily homicide, of course; it may be accident. It will depend on circumstances. We will go into the characteristics of entry and exit wounds in a moment. Suicidal wounds with a firearm are almost always contact wounds. Most suicides choose to shoot themselves in the head, right or left temple (left for left-handers), middle of the forehead, roof of the mouth, slides 6 and 7 please . . . and seven? Thank you. Note the characteristic cruciate form – split form – of the contact wound. The remainder choose to shoot themselves over the heart . . . Slide 8 please . . . Never in the face. As a general rule, a wound in the back or at some other inaccessible spot should always arouse your suspicion. But such are the vagaries of human nature that apparent homicide may, on close inspection, prove to be suicide, and there are cases on record where a shot . . . '

The lozenges of the front door quite dark, approaching. Rain outside, a cyclist passing in a shiny black mackintosh cape. Iridescent oil stains on the road.

Standing by the mortuary trolley he read the police report: 'Detective Inspector Albert Thudichum. At 11.40 a.m. on Friday 11 October in answer to a 999 call, I proceeded with Detective Sergeant Parker to 4 Murchison Mansions, Sinclair Street, W.1. On arrival a police ambulance was about to depart from the premises with occupant of Flat 4, Basil Mynford Forrest who, I was informed, had been shot. I was further informed that Forrest was alive but in a serious condition. On proceeding to the flat where said shooting had occurred I found Mrs Ada Lincoln, forty-five, of 6 Lydia Terrace, NW1, Mrs Rose Harris, forty-three, of 12 Cobb Road, NW11, cleaners, and Dr Walter Waite, eighty-two, of Flat 36 Murchison Mansions. Mrs Lincoln informed me that she had found the wounded man when she had arrived at approx 10.30 that morning as usual to clean the flat. She has been employed by Forrest for eighteen months.

'On finding Forrest on the floor, she immediately called Mrs Harris, her co-worker, and together they decided to summon Dr Waite who resides in the building. Dr Waite saw Forrest lying on living-room floor by fireplace, head nearest fireplace, right hand clasping an automatic. He was bleeding from a wound in the head, unconscious but still breathing. Dr Waite returned to his own flat on the top floor of Murchison Mansions and after an interval arrived back with swabs and certain

93

medical supplies. In the meantime, the two ladies wiped the blood from the wound. On his return, Dr Waite swabbed and cleaned the wound, dressed it and together with Mrs Lincoln and Mrs Harris made Forrest as comfortable as possible on the sofa, and Dr Waite then instructed Mrs Harris to go and call the police. Forrest remained unconscious.

'Dr J Janek of St William's Hospital states that an X-ray examination was performed and a bullet located in the skull. It was decided not to operate since it was considered that Forrest would not survive it and in fact he died without regaining consciousness at 10.15 the following night.

'From inquiries made it appears that Forrest, a bachelor, had no close relatives living except an aunt, Mrs Wynyfred Pertwee, residing at Hove. Mrs Pertwee states that she had broken off with deceased four years earlier after a dispute over money. Various letters of an affectionate type were found by Detective Sergeant Parker and these have led to interviews with five young women, none of whom can shed light on Forrest's death. Two of these, May Igglestone, twenty-eight, of 10 Hollycombe Terrace, SW2 and Doris Marsden, twenty-six, of 22A Henrietta Street, SE12, state that they had appointments with Forrest for the evening of his death and both are strongly of opinion that he was 'not the suicide type'. They knew him as 'a gentleman of private means' who had 'distinguished Society connections'. Mrs Lincoln states that young women often stayed overnight at the Murchison Mansions flat; she had not been paid for a fortnight at time of Forrest's demise.

'No suicide note was found and it has not so far been possible to reconstruct deceased's movements on the evening of shooting. None of occupants of the other flats, duly questioned, noticed anything amiss, though one, Mr Percy Catton, sixty-two, retired, occupant of second-floor flat, No 10, states there was an attempted burglary on that floor eighteen months ago, not reported to police at time.

'Dr Waite states that deceased had been shot in the back of the head behind right ear and this was confirmed by Dr J. Janek. In view of this, a strong suspicion of homicide must be entertained. Unfortunately neither Dr Waite nor the two charladies is able to say definitely if weapon was clasped tightly in deceased's hand or held loosely. Dr Waite, who seems to have removed the gun – a fact about which all three are confused – was at first affirmative that 'he was clutching it tight' but later less positive.

'No attempt had been made to rob the flat. Mrs Lincoln is not aware of any visitors due that evening but states that Forrest was irregular in his habits and did not inform her of his movements. She confirms that she found no unusual disorder; nothing appeared to be missing. The hospital reports that the sum of four pounds one shilling and two pence was found in Forrest's pocket.

'The front door of the flat is fitted with a Wembley 'Crown' lock, a well-known type which allows the catch to be taken off if a central knob is pushed in, and the door opened without a key. Mrs Lincoln states that Forrest sometimes left the door off the catch for her to come in without disturbing him. She states she thinks it was off the catch when she first went in and found the deceased shot.

'The weapon found is a .25 automatic of Italian make, four and a half inches long. The bullet has remained in the body pending the post-mortem. Forrest had no licence to possess a firearm.

'Drs J. Janek and W. Poole who examined Forrest at the hospital saw no powder marks either on the wound or on Forrest's hand. If any existed they may have been washed off either by Dr Waite or the two ladies or by hospital staff preparing Forrest for X-ray examination.

'A preliminary investigation of Forrest's affairs shows that he was in serious financial straits with debts of nine hundred and four pounds. Letters from two solicitors threatening legal action to recover outstanding bills were found. Mrs Lincoln states she has seen plenty of others but that Forrest 'never worried about money.' On the theory of homicide it appears certain that Forrest opened the door or left it open for someone he knew, at all events somebody he trusted enough to turn his back on at a critical moment. Inquiries are continuing.

'In view of above, District Coroner was informed and gave

95

instructions for deceased to be removed to coroner's mortuary, North-West Paddington District for post-mortem and
inquest.'

Bowen was not the most difficult coroner in London nor yet
the most predictable. He was a tall bald man with a small
moustache, the army-colonel type. 'Sir Bertram Pendleton.
Please state your position and qualifications.'

'I am a Doctor of Medicine and Surgery of the University of
London, a Member of the Royal College of Physicians,
London, Lecturer on Special Pathology at St Edward's Hospi-
tal, London, Lecturer on Medical Jurisprudence at St Paul's
Infirmary. I have wide experience of medico-legal work. I have
read the police report and heard the evidence given here by Dr
Waite, Dr Janek, Dr Poole and Dr Carr who saw, all of them
saw, the deceased at St William's Hospital.

'On 22 October I examined, in the presence of Detective
Inspector Thudichum – I examined the body at Paddington
mortuary. Deceased was a well-nourished man of thirty-nine.
I found a perforating wound in the skull one and a half inches
behind the right ear caused by a bullet. The wound was small
and well-defined. It had a circumference of less than a quarter-
inch. The edges were reddish but there was practically no
destruction of tissue at the entry site. Otherwise – deceased
was otherwise uninjured, except for a bruise on the nose
caused when falling into the fireplace.

'On opening the skull I found the brain membranes in-
flamed and purulent matter present. The bullet – I should first
say the dura mater had been punctured. The bullet was em-
bedded in the bone of the base of the skull close to the sphe-
noid bone about an inch and a half behind the entry site. The
direction of the bullet was horizontal and from behind for-
wards; it had a downward, a slight downward, inclination.
The cavity round the heart was healthy, the lungs and air
passages were clean. The liver weighed 1.612 grammes and
was congested; the spleen was small and weighed 92
grammes. Both kidneys were congested and there was marked
stenosis of the left artery.'

'Did you make any later examination?'

'Yes. Microscopically there was much fatty degeneration of the liver and disease of arteries in the kidneys which had resulted in part of the kidney substances being wasted.'

'Were these, any of these things, an immediate threat to life?'

'No. The condition may have been due to alcoholic excess.'

'What was your conclusion as to the cause of death?'

'The direct cause of death was meningitis which had developed very rapidly as the result of the bullet wound.'

'How can the wound in the head be accounted for, in your opinion?'

'In my opinion, it was self-inflicted.'

Bowen shifted his papers, pushed his glasses further on to his nose. 'You have heard Dr Carr – Dr Wilfred Carr – and in this he is joined by Dr Pennefeather – say that in his opinion the position of the wound excludes any possibility of suicide. Dr Carr says that for the deceased to have shot himself in this way he would have had to place himself in a most awkward and unnatural position – that to do so he would have had to strain his arm back behind the shoulder. Dr Carr's word was 'inconceivable'. What do you say to that?' Bowen raised his eyebrows, rubbed his chin with his hand.

'I have had other cases of people shooting themselves behind the ear. With a small weapon such as this it would be perfectly easy . . . perfectly easy to hold it behind the head. Because of its light weight it would not place any strain on the person holding it . . . like this. Even a person who had no practice at using such a weapon would be able to hold it easily and naturally in such a position. There would be no real difficulty in getting the hand back from the head two or three inches, even more.'

Bowen said, 'But isn't it the reason why suicides – why people who shoot themselves – almost always put the weapon on the skin or close to the skin – isn't it because they are afraid of firing a shot that is not fatal, of just wounding themselves? The farther away, the greater the risk? Why run the risk?'

Sir Bertram Pendleton said, 'They usually hold it close to. But many do not like the feel of the barrel on the skin and so

97

they hold it away. Moreover, if the head is moved at the instant the trigger is pulled, this brings the head further away from the weapon to a certain extent. I mean, the person instinctively flinches and turns the head away from the nozzle and this would cause the bullet to go in a forward line and bring the point of entry further back in the head. The head might easily turn 30 degrees or more to produce such an angle. Similarly, a slight shift of the head would make all the difference to the upward or downward direction of the bullet.'

'But with respect, Sir Bertram, that is pure conjecture, is it not?'

'I think there must always be a degree of conjecture if no one is there to see what happens – conjecture based on scientific observation by a trained and experienced eye.'

Bowen cleared his throat. A reporter at the side was writing busily. 'Dr Waite says he is now fairly sure the deceased was not gripping the weapon very tightly. Doesn't this increase the possibility that the suicide was staged?'

'Suicides sometimes relax their grip at the moment of death. When you think of it, it is not surprising.'

'But why should anyone bent on suicide choose that particular site – the back of the head?'

'It is always difficult to be definite, one does not know. Women rarely shoot themselves in the head. A man, too, who is good-looking, as in this case, may not wish to disfigure himself. We are reduced to pure supposition – as so often.'

'Is the wound, then, in your opinion, consistent with suicide?'

'Oh quite.'

'Would you agree that you can get a wound that has all the appearance of a homicidal wound and that yet may be a suicidal wound?'

'Certainly.'

'And vice versa?'

'Suicidal wounds may have all the appearance of homicidal wounds. It is obviously not necessarily true that any homicidal wound may be a suicidal wound.'

'But you may get a wound in such a position as suggests homicide while in reality it is suicidal?'

'That is what I have been explaining. The head is the site of homicidal and suicidal wounds.'

Bowen paused a moment, then said, 'I would like to look at the question of motive. Apart from the debts, deceased appears to have had no motive for ending his life, he had previous – previous debts do not seem to have worried him. He had even made plans for that same evening. Is it . . . is it your experience that a person can behave in a perfectly sane way and suddenly commit suicide for no apparent motive?'

'There is usually a motive for suicide. But the most serious motives are usually unknown. Really disturbing worries are not talked about, they are kept private.'

'Thank you, Sir Bertram.'

The usual coughing and shuffling in court while Bowen pushed his glasses further on to his nose, scratched his head with the end of his pen, sifted through his notes, considered them. One of the jurors had a note passed to him; Bowen read it and nodded. At last he looked up. 'I think we have examined all aspects of this case on the . . . ah . . . the facts in our possession. We have had the benefit of Sir Bertram Pendleton's expert and experienced opinion. He has fully explained the reasons why he considers this a case of suicide and I think the jury will have been impressed by his arguments. I am not satisfied that we have got to the bottom of the case and I will adjourn the verdict to permit the police to further their inquiries.'

Surprise!

8

Miss Melanie Chitty, the library assistant, had made it clear at the time that having Inspector Kilburn examining the names and records and loitering about the Library with that ginger-haired young man, made her exceedingly uncomfortable. It had brought her nervous rash out on her neck and she had been relieved when the visits ceased. This afternoon, there-fore, she had let the Inspector in again to see Mr Lightfoot, the new librarian, with no pleasure. Glancing at the clock – they had been together in Mr Lightfoot's office now for twenty-five minutes – she hoped it wasn't going to begin all over again. She concentrated on the cards before her, trying to put the thing out of her mind; but before she could quite succeed, Mr Lightfoot himself appeared, came into the staff area and said he would take temporary charge of the ins and outs, Inspector Kilburn wished to see her in his office.

With a little moistening of her lips, Miss Chitty rose and walked round. She paused outside the door to collect herself, straightening her dress, then knocked. The Inspector, stand-ing by Mr Lightfoot's desk, had a pipe in his hand. She had difficulty in looking straight at him. Could she say whether this was Mr Leopold Cox's pipe? No. Would she kindly exam-ine it more closely? Hadn't she at the time of the original inquiry said that Mr Cox smoked a pipe with a silver band round it like this one had? Yes . . . Perhaps this was the pipe? It looked like it. Had she often seen Mr Cox smoking it? Occasionally, only in his office. Couldn't she be sure? She took no particular notice of pipes. It might be this or another. Well, there were not all that number of pipes with silver bands, were there? She really couldn't say. She would remember that at the time he had asked if Mr Cox had left any other pipes behind in the Library. Yes, she remembered; he had not. So she could say this might well be the pipe? Yes. Although she wasn't looking at the Inspector, she knew he was scrutinizing her closely. Wasn't there something else she wished to tell him? No. A small detail she had perhaps forgotten before? No. A pause. The Inspector thanked her, that was all for the time being.

Miss Chitty was sure the Inspector had, in some police fashion, learned that she knew about Mr Cox and Miss Pendleton; that she, Melanie Chitty, had committed a criminal offence by not speaking of it and that for some reason he wanted to prolong her distress before charging her . . . leading her away in handcuffs in front of Mr Lightfoot, before she had time to collect her handbag . . . She also wanted to ask why the inquiries were continuing when the verdict had been accidental death, but of course she was far too nervous to do so.

Ivy had turned the light on in the kitchen since it was prematurely dark and the rain continued to fall steadily. Mrs Tickner had kept her talking most of the afternoon and, although by staying in the kitchen instead of going through into the living-room Ivy had hoped to encourage Mrs Tickner to leave, this stratagem had failed, Mrs Tickner had used the rain as an excuse to stay on, and as the hour passed and then another, the dark-brown dregs of tea cold in the bottom of the cups, Ivy had become progressively less sure of herself or of why Mrs Tickner was there.

The conversation kept alighting on Boudie, Mrs Tickner persisting in a steady pressure of questions. It had given Ivy a throbbing headache. She felt intolerably oppressed. The light accentuated the stringiness of Mrs Tickner's neck, the dark gap of her mouth. She kept asking why Ivy had looked after Boudie so devotedly all these years, sacrificing herself, her own life. What had Ivy left out? Eh? What was the real reason?

In the end, after a great struggle with herself, Ivy murmured, 'I promised Mother . . . I . . . I promised to . . . to look after him . . . to protect him.'

'Oh yes, I know all about that. I know about that, my dear.'

'You do . . . ?'

'Yes, yes. All about it. You can tell me the rest, I won't say a word, don't worry.'

'Leo? The librarian . . . ?'

'The – wait . . .' For a second, Mrs Tickner stumbled. 'The one who was found dead in – ?'

Ivy nodded.' He . . . he did . . . he was naughty.'

Mrs Tickner stretched out a reassuring hand. 'My dear, how strange, that was exactly your mother's phrase, your mother's expression. Oh, my dear, you musn't worry . . . I'm as silent as the grave. Your mother would have told you so. So it wasn't an accident? He did it? Boudie? . . . I won't say a word, my dear.'

'You won't, will you?'

'You can trust me. Tell me . . . The police were suspicious but I'm your friend.'

'I've *had* to worry. What . . . what would happen to him if Ivy got married? Did you ever think of that? Ivy has looked after him all these years. She had to.'

'Oh, I've known as much all along. I've known a lot of things and never breathed a word, never a word, so you see you can trust me. I'm on your side. I knew he wasn't right, you know.'

'You did?'

'Oh, I knew he wasn't right long ago. Of course I did.'

'Without Ivy he would be . . . be worse. He wouldn't be able to keep control of himself . . . and . . . and do all that work. Without Ivy he'd be lost.'

Eagerly Mrs Tickner nodded.

'He'd give himself away . . . wouldn't be able to help himself. Ivy wouldn't be there to protect him. He – '

'Yes, go on.'

'He's been getting reckless.'

'When was that? Tell me. Wait – the night I came in and you were boiling those clothes, you remember that? You said they were Boudie's working aprons; I could see they weren't aprons; and even if they had been the hospital would have laundered them. That was something, was it?'

'Yes.'

'Something else he'd done. Been reckless?'

Ivy nodded, looking distantly across the room.

'And what – I've often thought about it – what if the man you married found out about him? He wouldn't be like me,' Mrs Tickner said. 'Wouldn't keep quiet, eh? Wouldn't be on your side, eh?'

'Boudie would have to get rid of him. Ivy knew that.'

'You couldn't take him to live with you and your new husband? What a nightmare!'

'No! No!'

'Can you imagine it? Perhaps you did imagine it?'

'Most of the time he was quiet . . . ' Ivy said.

'Oh, my dear, perhaps you don't realize it. He's always looked strange. "Wobbly" we used to call him, "Wobbly". When my dear Stanley was alive we used to look out of the window and we'd say, "Did you see Wobbly leave the house this morning?"'

'That wasn't kind,' Ivy said.

'And that horrible profession . . . putting his nose into dead bodies, ugh! But he's an important person, Sir Bertram this, Sir Bertram that (mimicking), your mother used to say so grandly.' Hastily Mrs Tickner changed her tone, leaned forward reassuringly. 'My dear, you know I'm on your side. The other times, tell me about that; when he wasn't quiet, eh? Tell me.'

'Sometimes my friends . . .'

'Yes, your friends?'

'Yes, the men . . . the ones who tried to make up to Ivy . . . He's always kept them away.'

'How do you mean?'

'Got them out of the way.'

'Yes . . . accidents, like . . . like Leo?'

'Or . . .'

'Yes, yes, I understand so well . . . men who became too friendly?'

'Yes.'

'Got rid of them?'

'M'mm.'

'I've guessed it. Oh, I've guessed it from what your mother

used to say. You couldn't look at a man. Worse than a jealous sweetheart! Much worse! And your mother knew, didn't she?'

'Yes.'

'She used to tell me things. She used to . . . When she was upset she used to say to me, "Oh dear, Mrs Tickner, what shall I do about Boudie?" She confided in me, used to put her hand on my arm, said he'd been naughty. What had he done, eh? You can trust me. What was it he did? I can keep a secret. Lots of people can't. Your mother used to say in strict confidence, "I can unburden myself to you, Maud. It makes me feel stronger."'

'I'm sure Mother never – '

'That's just where you're mistaken, my dear. Quite mistaken. She used to lay her hand on my arm in absolute trust. Your mother always confided in me. There was something about six months before your mother died. What was that? Something – your mother was very upset.'

'No . . . nothing . . . ' Ivy had both hands overlapping on her chest, hardly able to breathe. Mrs Tickner was transformed, on edge with excitement. Weakly Ivy wanted to plead with her to stop, to clasp her knees.

'What's upstairs? What does he do upstairs, eh? That bumping sound? What does he do? It's something, I know. It's a good job I'm a sympathetic friend, isn't it? It's a good job I'm a person with principles, a lady, a person of breeding, eh? Now take me upstairs and show me what he does. It's in his bedroom, isn't it? Come along, take me up now.'

Gripping Ivy's arm, Mrs Tickner pulled her tremblingly to her feet. Ivy's resistance had collapsed; Mrs Tickner led her out of the kitchen towards the stairs. They groped in the half-dark, knocked something over with a crash, found the light switch and, with Mrs Tickner heaving and hauling, they stumbled up the stairs. On the landing, Mrs Tickner released her grip, darted forward as if she had long ago worked out the geography of the house, similar to her own, in any event, and before Ivy could react, flung the bedroom door wide open with a vibrant bang. There was a second of darkness while she found the switch then she let out an exclamation and her face became illumined with triumphant, malicious joy. *'There!*

105

That's it! There it is!' Advancing into the room she gave a loud laugh, her open mouth showing her gap-toothed lower gums. One outstretched hand on the horse's head, she stood back surveying it in mockery, walked round it, turned to Ivy, her eyes glowing. 'Go on! It's your turn – get on for a ride. Yes! Yes! Go on, get on for a ride!'

'No . . . Don't . . . No . . . ' Ivy pulled weakly away from her grip, Mrs Tickner dragged her forward, pressed her against the horse, reached down trying to catch Ivy's leg, grappled with her and half-tipped Ivy over. Ivy, lying awkwardly half across the horse like a sack, tried to resist, then yielded and let Mrs Tickner haul and push one leg over, tearing her skirt and at once Mrs Tickner was rocking the horse furiously back and forth, slapping its rump, darting in front with neck outstretched to urge Ivy on, laughing and calling out, 'Tally-hoo!'

Jerked to and fro, Ivy clung to the horse's neck, the runners thumped loudly on the floor. The wardrobe rocked and the glass-fronted door creaked jerkily open with the vibration. At last Mrs Tickner stopped pushing, the horse slowed down and Ivy slid breathlessly off, tearing her dress further. She collapsed on the bed, buried her face in her arms. Mrs Tickner had momentarily dropped her and was inspecting the bedroom. She saw Teddy on the bed and snatched it up with another howl, flung it back. From the wardrobe she lifted out the freshly laundered tutu and red tights on a hanger, gave another bleat of joy. She held them up in front of herself, dropped them and stood over Ivy. 'Well, it's all true, isn't it? Eh? It's all true?'

Not looking up, Ivy nodded her head; deep sobs shook her, her hairpins had come out and her hair straggled over her face and shoulders. She sobbed with bent shoulders. At last, sniffing and snuffling she subsided, pushed back her hair, uncovered her wet red face. When she could speak she said, 'You won't tell anybody, will you? He's not . . . he doesn't know . . . he's not . . . you won't, will you?' She sat up, searching for a handkerchief, wiped her face with the bottom of her dress, found a handkerchief, blew her nose.

'Oh, Mrs Tickner,' Ivy's puffed face looked pleadingly up, 'I've been wrong about you all these years. You're really good

106

and kind. You understand . . . you understand, don't you?'

Mrs Tickner seemed taller, no longer her earlier self.

'Oh dear . . . !' Abruptly Ivy's eyes filled with alarm and she got to her feet. 'We can't stay here. Boudie'll be home any minute!'

Mrs Tickner sobered at once, busied towards the door. 'I think I left my keys in the kitchen.' They shut the bedroom door behind them. 'Don't worry,' Mrs Tickner said. 'What you need tonight is a good sleep. I know it's early but this has been a strain for you. Why don't you go to bed, eh? Straight to bed, go on, I'll pop in in the morning.'

'I think I'll have to, I've got a splitting headache.'

They went down the stairs.

Sir Bertram Pendleton let himself in by the front door, hung up his hat and coat, dropped his bag and looked into the living-room. Nobody there; the light came from the kitchen. He went through. Ivy was sprawled at the table, her face red, her hair half down. He stepped hastily forward and in alarm bent over her. 'My dear . . . my dear, what's happened? What's the matter . . . ? Tell me? What's upset you?'

She shook her head in silence. Stabbed by love, he sat down on the chair next to her, put his arm over her shoulder, stroked back her hair and kissed her cheek. 'What's the matter, my dear? Let me help you. I'm here now, everything's all right. There's nothing to worry about.'

She fiddled with her hearing aid, turned her blue eyes on him, the blue eyes he had always thought so lovely when she was a girl, that still filled him with tenderness.

'Tell me.'

'Mrs Tickner.'

'What about her? She's been here?'

'She knows . . . she . . .'

'Knows? She's been here upsetting you?'

'Knows all about it. Everything . . .'

'No, no, my darling. You mustn't fret. You mustn't worry yourself. There's nothing to worry about. You look tired; perhaps you should go to bed, have an early night. Will you? Take one of your pills, h'm?' He sat holding her against him, talking to her quietly, soothing her. At length he said, 'Is she there now, next door, Mrs Tickner?'

Ivy did not answer and he got to his feet. Abruptly and unexpectedly she stood up too and said dryly, in a voice that did not seem to match her mood, 'Yes . . . I will.'

He hung fire for a moment, uncertain, then led her with his arm round her waist to the foot of the stairs and, after watching her go up, strode into the kitchen and out by the back door.

The dark garden was soggy with water. The gap in the fence separating the two houses, always used by the Tickners for calls, was half-blocked by the forsythia bush; he pushed through. A light showed in the Tickners' kitchen. The glass panel of the door rattled loosely under his rap; he expected Mrs Tickner to open to him, but instead she called out from inside in an affected voice, 'Oh do come in, won't you?' He turned the brass knob, went in.

Mrs Tickner was stationed under the pendant light in a brown wig, her mouth enlarged by lipstick. Lifting one shoulder, she extended her arm, offering her hand. 'How do you do, Sir Bertram?' From somewhere she had dug out a pink low-waisted 'twenties frock with knee-length pleated skirt; a string of turquoise beads dangled to her waist.

'Good evening. You have been talking to my sister, I think?'

'Yes, we had a little chat.'

'What have you been saying to her?'

'It's what she's been saying to me.' She sidled up to him, smiling. 'I knew you'd come, I've been waiting for you. You're going to have to marry me, Bertram.'

He stared, dumb.

'Lady Pendleton.' Hand on one hip, she swayed. 'Suits me splendidly, h'm? The Opera – Royal Ascot and Glorious Goodwood, of course. Photographs in *The Tatler*, with A. N. Other.'

'What are you talking about?'

'I happen to know certain things – oh, I'd guessed them you know. Oh yes, we haven't been next-door neighbours all these years for nothing.'

'Certain things? Such as what?'

She stretched both arms downwards, one palm pressed in the other, a girlish gesture. 'Oh . . . the death . . . the so-called accident to the librarian, for one.'

'So-called? Why?'

She giggled. 'Oh no . . . You don't think I'm going to tell you what I know. That would be silly, wouldn't it?'

'If you know something about it, you should tell the police.'

'I think I may have to.'

'Is this what you've been discussing with my poor sister?'

'Bertram, your poor sister, as you call her – you should have thought of her sooner. Now it's too late. She can't stand it any more. She's got to relieve her mind. And not only to me.'

'But with your help, I suppose?'

'What's that?' She turned her head rapidly at a small sound from outside, stepped swiftly past him and snatched the back door open; but apparently there was nothing there and she shut it again. 'That was my cat – that you frightened away. It smelt you were here.'

'Aren't you being ridiculous, Mrs Tickner?'

'Oh, the grand manner won't wash with me, Bertram. I know too much. The librarian . . . I was at the inquest, you know. The inquest, yes! And the police didn't seem to think it was an accident. You remember?'

'But the verdict was accidental death. If you were to suggest otherwise, you would expose yourself to a very serious charge.'

'You won't intimidate me, Bertram!'

'Do you think they'd believe your word against mine?'

'But you remember they were looking for an Italian or an Australian. What if I told them you are Boudie? H'm? Boudie – that would ring a bell, wouldn't it? They were looking for an intruder called Bodi or Bondi. Besides, they'd have Ivy's word too.' Mrs Tickner turned for the door. 'I shouldn't have left her alone tonight . . .'

He shot out his arm held the door shut. 'She is upset enough already, Mrs Tickner. You . . . Listen . . . listen to me, try to understand. My sister is not always herself. She doesn't realize what she's saying. She – '

'Oh, you want to explain to me now, h'm?'

'She – I ask you to listen, Mrs Tickner – at times she confuses things, confuses people, mixes herself up with other people. It

109

may sound improbable to you – impossible – but it is quite real – the boundary between herself and others, between what she does and what other people do, particularly between what she does and what I do is . . . is . . . vague – tenuous – uncertain. To her the line between us is sometimes indistinguishable. A violent event she transfers immediately since it is connected with strong emotion . . . and she . . . she transfers it most easily to me, because I am nearest to her.'

'You are trying to shift the blame to her – to say she's the mad one, not you. She's been keeping you out of trouble for years. I know more than you think, you see. Oh yes, much more. There were others, weren't there, besides the librarian? Eh? Weren't there? Every time Ivy had a man friend, you had to get him out of the way.'

'That is what she told you?'

'She did!'

'By that she meant "so-called accidents" and, I suppose "so-called suicides". Is that it?'

'She didn't mention suicides – but that's what you called them! It shows you knew all about them, doesn't it?' She rocked herself in triumph.

'But my dear Mrs Tickner, why should I do these things? Did she tell you that?'

'Yes. Because you were afraid. You knew that without her there would be nobody to protect you – the great Sir Bertram Pendleton, mad! You imagine? Mad!'

'And how was she protecting me?'

Mrs Tickner hesitated, twitched her mouth impatiently.

He said, 'By eliminating the men who threatened to take her away from me and leave me defenceless. That's what she was doing – isn't that what she said? It's strange reasoning, isn't it? But people who are not sane reason strangely. And, you notice, it's a transfer of the truth about herself.'

'The truth about her – about – *Ivy*? It was Ivy? Is that what you're – ? But she has been sacrificing herself for you – she promised her mother – she says – '

'Of course she does. It's what she believes – profoundly believes it. It is her system . . . her . . . her fantasy. And if this . . . this protection fantasy breaks down, she'll . . . she'll go

110

over the top. Alas, the system is self-perpetuating, she's kept the fantasy alive by constantly trying to find another man. Fortunately, she is no longer young.'

Mrs Tickner said, 'That rocking horse you've got upstairs, then, in your room, who rides that? Eh? Tell me. And the teddy bear and the – they're your things, Bertram. You can't deny – '

'But those things, Mrs Tickner – I can hardly expect you to understand – I've been playing up to her. Those things are part of the deception that I'm the guilty one, the props, the costume. Every time I ride the rocking horse it reinforces her belief that it's me – that she's strong and loved – needed – brave and good and protective: it comforts her, calms her down, helps me to keep her relatively – '

'Oh, it's too – how can I tell you're not trying to deceive me?'

'You can't. You'll have to trust me.' He paused. 'Mrs Tickner, I can't send her to Broadmoor.'

'Then find somewhere else'. Her voice was still sharp with suspicion. 'You must send her somewhere else – a well-run home, quiet, private. You know where those places are . . . you can find one.'

'But then I shouldn't be able to help her. That's why I'm with her as much as I can be.'

'If you are telling the truth, she should be locked up!'

'Broadmoor? No. And if you denounce her to the police, it will be the end of – of – '

'Oh the end of you . . . the end of your career. And that's your main concern, isn't it?'

'No . . . no, it is not. But . . . you will make sure of never being Lady Pendleton.'

She cocked her head, regarded him obliquely, twitching her lips. 'So then, otherwise, we shall be married, Bertram?'

He gazed back at her, finally said, 'Very well.' At her smile, he added, 'Ivy will have to be part of the household.'

Mrs Tickner's look changed. 'No . . . no . . . that is not possible. No. So there's no choice. I might have known. I shall go to the police in the morning.'

'I beg you not to do that, Mrs Tickner. We can see more of each other, learn to know each other, value each other, even

. . . who knows . . . ? There are many things we can talk over, choices open to us. And, after all, *you* will be Lady Pendleton.'

Illumination broke slowly over Mrs Tickner, she seemed to see distant islands of gold, glowing, beckoning. She straightened her back, lifted her chin. 'Your solemn word?'

'Yes.'

'Maud. You may kiss me.'

The rain was still falling in the garden. Gently, Sir Bertram Pendleton let himself into the kitchen, locked the door and window, threw the keys on the table and passed his hand over his face, exhausted. He paused, then reaching into the cupboard, he took out the flagon of Emu and poured himself three-quarters of a glassful.

The lamp in the living-room made a wedge of light on the hall and stairs. Carrying the glass he went up until he could see Ivy's bedroom door; it was shut, the light out. He retreated softly to the living-room, sank down with a sigh in his armchair, took a drink of the wine, screwing up his lips, placed the glass on the small rectangular table beside him. He let his head rest against the back of the chair, his gaze did not rise to the family photographs on the mantelpiece. The rain seemed to have lessened, the intervals between the drips became wider.

In the morning he was up first as usual, made the tea and took a cup to Ivy upstairs. The room was in semi-darkness, the curtains were drawn, she was still sleeping; he made out her head in the upheaval of bedclothes and as he moved round quietly, balancing the cup, to place it on the bedside table, he saw that her face was puffed and unnaturally blotchy. He put the tea down. One of her hands showed; gently he lifted it, she did not stir; pulse and breathing were normal but he felt uneasy about her. The turmoil of the bed indicated a bad night. He stood looking down at her, then crept out.

In the kitchen he paused as something came back to him. Wait a minute . . . When he had thrown the kitchen keys on the table last night, there had been something else there – the teapot, yes . . . and two other keys on a ring. Two other keys. Had he put them somewhere without thinking? He moved round scanning the kitchen; they were no longer there.

The soft grey morning light came in through the door-panel and the window. He stood gazing out at the brilliantly green stretch of grass, the dripping, drooping, buffeted beds of flowers. A starling alighted on a slender branch and flew off again, releasing a shower of drops.

Mrs Tickner!

9

'Oh, the usual thing, sir – the milk-bottles.' Police Sergeant Yates scratched his chin with his thumb. 'Side-window left open about six inches, on the catch, one of them rods, you know. We had to break the pane to get in. Coroner's officer'll be here shortly – you know Sergeant Cooch, sir?'

'Oh yes,' Sir Bertram Pendleton said.

'Right on your doorstep, this one.'

'Yes, lucky to have you handy, Sir Bertram,' the police doctor said. 'You'll be doing the PM?'

'I can't do anything without the coroner's order. It's entirely up to him. I must be very careful not to interfere – you know the regulations and you know Mr Dysart.'

'I do indeed, Sir Bertram. Still, what I mean is I'm glad to have your opinion.'

'On the face of it, she fell downstairs. Maybe a break in the cervical vertebrae – I wouldn't like to say more at this stage.'

'Quite so, Sir Bertram. There's a stair-rod loose at the top, they say.'

'Which may not be the cause of the fall, of course.'

'Naturally not.'

'You acquainted with the lady, by any chance, Sir Bertram?' the Sergeant said.

'No . . . no, not really. A next-door neighbour basis, you know. We've been neighbours for many years; but not more, no.'

'Any particular problems, you know?'

'I know nothing of her private affairs, Sergeant. Simply a neighbour. You say the place was locked up?'

115

'Oh yes. Kitchen door locked from inside, front door shut – have to have a key to get in, and the key was on her bunch. No sign of illegal entry or anything of that sort.'

'I see.'

'Her bed's been slept in. She seems to have gone to bed, turned the light on and got up for something. Detective Inspector Kilburn is on his way round.'

'Well – let me know if you need me.'

'Thank you, Sir Bertram.'

Sir Bertram Pendleton had not used the club more than a dozen times in the last ten years and regularly, once a year when it came to paying his fees, wondered why he kept it up; but for some reason he always had. This morning the main dining-room was full and they were using the small room for the overflow. He spotted Dr Wilfred Carr at the table for two from which another member was just rising, leaving the second place. Sir Bertram went up: 'Good morning. Mind if I join you? We seem to be rather busy this morning.'

Carr looked up and said, 'Good morning,' dryly; he was already half-way through his steak and kidney pie. He wore a yellow tie with blue dots; his hair was stuck down on his head. The waiter (they wouldn't have girls serving) cleared the place and set out fresh things. Sir Bertram ordered. The waiter said, 'Sorry, sir, we don't have Emu.' Sir Bertram noticed Carr's smirk and said, 'Never mind, then.'

They exchanged a spare phrase or two, then Sir Bertram said, 'I hear Dysart's put you on that case next door to me.'

Carr looked surprised and irritated. 'I heard you'd been looking at it.'

'Oh . . . the police happened to tell me just after they had found her, that's all. Have you done the PM yet?'

'I have, yes. Putting in my report in the morning.'

'Murder, undoubtedly.'

Carr stopped chewing; his eyes looked smaller when his eyebrows were raised. 'Oh?'

'Clear from her attitude. She was pitched down the stairs.'

'Did you examine the body?'

'I was careful not to touch it. The police were there, the police surgeon was there.'

In a hostile tone, Carr said, 'Then I don't see how, from a superficial look at the body at the foot of the stairs, you can give any opinion at all, let alone decide she was murdered.'

'In my experience people who fall downstairs in a house break a limb or a hip but don't kill themselves. People who are killed are pushed.'

'Your experience is enough to tell you that?' Carr snorted. 'Forgive me if I'm sceptical.'

'The woman was obviously pushed from behind and at the bottom of the stairs – the carpet was too thin to provide any protection – her head was lifted up and dashed against the edge of the bottom step to make sure of fatal injury. The injury I noticed under the chin indicated that one of the blows snapped her head back and probably dislocated the spine. The curved shape of the outer wound corresponded to the curvature of the step. It is obviously murder.'

Carr dabbed his mouth with his napkin. 'Sir Bertram, the blind conviction that you are right and everybody else is wrong is well known. I don't share it. You have absolutely no evidence of anything but a fall. The shaped wound she would get when her head struck the bottom step. There is also – which you evidently didn't notice – the mark of the angle of the banister post.'

'She was in her nightdress and – '

'But she'd been in bed, for God's sake!' Carr was beginning to heat up.

'Yes, but there was a peculiar formation of the hair – it was bunched up where somebody had gripped her by the hair to lift her head and bang it down again.'

'You're always so certain. You deal in cast-iron certainties. It's amazing! Forgive me, Sir Bertram, but I think you are talking nonsense. How is it that you are always seeing something that nobody else can see? It's like the famous bruise in the Snow case – bruise on the dead woman's larynx. Three other pathologists – top men, very *experienced* men – examined the body and when they couldn't find the bruise you simply said it had disappeared! But the man who was supposed to have caused it was hanged!'

The waiter looked startled. One or two other lunchers glanced round curiously.

Pendleton said, 'But my dear young man, why should she get up in the middle of the night? I'm told her bedroom light was on. She heard something, and didn't realize the murderer was standing behind her about to pitch her down the stairs.'

'A murderer who doesn't steal anything? Doesn't disturb anything? Who gets in without forcing an entry – hardly likely to be a friendly visitor, somebody she knew, whom she would receive in her nightgown. How do you account for it?'

'Somebody was hiding in the house or came in through the kitchen door before she locked it.'

Carr made a contemptuous little explosion of his lips. 'Then hid till she was in bed? What for? And left, locking the door behind him? Doesn't make sense.'

'No. Simply left and slammed the front door after him.'

'Murderers usually leave by the front door in your experience, especially when there is also a safer back door? Forgive me, Sir Bertram, I believe in being direct. This is the sort of thing you've got away with for far too long. It's become notorious, in fact it's become a scandal. You come along and say, "I saw such and such and this is what happened," and they all swallow it, police, judges, juries, counsel, swallow anything you say. Yet you've made mistake after mistake! The Forrest case – so-called suicide. The Ferguson case. You make some worthless gun tests, you give out that the evidence is perfectly consistent with the man's wife having shot herself in the head (though there was absolutely no reason for her to do so), that in your *incomparable* experience it's either suicide or at the most accident, you pooh-pooh contrary evidence by Redpath and others, with the result that the man is acquitted – and fifteen months later, after committing another murder, he kills himself and leaves a note confessing he shot his wife. The – the librarian case: it may interest you to know that the police found the dead man's missing pipe near the golf links after that so-called accident . . . what was the man's name? Yes, Cox. I suppose he threw it away before he went home and slipped in the bathroom?

'And you go on as large as life, as certain as ever. Well, it's not going to happen in this case. And I am going to warn Dysart. But tell me this – why are you so interested in this case? It's curious . . . it's strange.'

'My next-door neighbour, if you don't mind!'

'Well, I'd say there was something else too, Sir Bertram. A tinge of professional jealousy. No? Instead of calling in the celebrated Sir Bertram Pendleton, although he is just next door, the coroner gives the case to me. You think you've been snubbed. Go on, admit it! And as a matter of fact, I think you have been!'

'You'll have to explain why this woman simply fell down the stairs in the middle of the night – and you have no explanation, my young friend.'

'Oh I haven't, haven't I? Well, since it can't change anything, I'll tell you. Perfectly simple. Your supposed murderer was a cat. A cat, sir! How do you like that? The woman got out of bed because she thought she heard her cat come back. Detective Inspector Kilburn has been very thorough, done excellent work. He has been going round and he has found out that she had been asking all the neighbours and local shop-keepers if they had seen her cat. She left a side window open just wide enough for the cat to climb in if it came back – and she left food out and kept it renewed. A stray cat got in, found the food and couldn't get out again. Mrs Tickner heard it and got up. Have you ever seen a heavy, full-grown cat that is fright-ened in a confined space and can't find its way out? Terrifying! Great frantic leaps and bounds – ten – twelve feet off the floor. And dangerous! It must have scared the life out of her. At the very *least* it got under her feet – but there were scratches on her neck and we think it must have leapt on her – and she fell.'

'I maintain that it is a case of murder. I shall not change my mind,' Sir Bertram Pendleton said.

'But you never do, do you? Let me tell you something, Sir Bertram. You sat down here with the idea of influencing me. Oh yes you did, don't deny it. I say nothing about the impro-priety – perhaps that will arise later. I haven't, as a matter of fact, written my report yet. But if I'd had any doubts, any doubts at all, they would have been entirely dispelled by this conversation. I am ten times stronger in my conviction that it was an accident. And that's that! Good-day to you.'

He rose triumphantly and stalked out.

'Cheese, sir?' the waiter inserted himself into the awkward interval and solicitously asked.

'Er . . . please,' Sir Bertram said.

'A glass of wine with it, perhaps, sir? We don't have the Emu, but we do have the Cassowary, From New Zealand, sir. Very nice.'

'Yes, that sounds splendid.' Sir Bertram Pendleton leaned back in pleasurable anticipation.

Miss Meecham's small spicy-smelling general store and post office was busy. Three customers from the village chatted among themselves on one side, waiting their turn. Miss Meecham was single-handed and not quick.

'. . . and a ball of string,' Ivy said. 'Oh and a quarter of tea. That'll be all, Miss Meecham.'

Mild-faced refined Miss Meecham (bun and glasses) disappeared behind the ramparts of goods on the counter, bobbed into view again, smiled. 'I must say it's fresh for May, isn't it?'

'I need a shilling postal order too, but – ' Ivy glanced round at the three other women, 'never mind for now, I'll come back.'

Sir Bertram Pendleton was gazing at the tall glass jars of sweets on the counter in front of the panel showing Mr Kruschen gaily leaping another hurdle to health. 'What do they call these?' he said.

'Those? They're pear-drops, Sir Bertram. Great favourites.'

'And these?'

'Those are the ones that change colour.' Miss Meecham simpered. 'The boys . . . (she half-concealed her face with a refined hand) . . . the boys call them "gob-stoppers". It sounds awfully vulgar but I'm told it is a perfectly respectable word. Colonel Firebrace says it's from the Gaelic and means one's mouth, you know.'

'Ah . . . ' Sir Bertram Pendleton nodded, and at that

120

moment caught Ivy's eye resting on the young man with a plump face, wearing a cap and bicycling clips on his trousers, who had just come in. Reddening self-consciously, the young man edged towards a corner.

Firmly Sir Bertram took Ivy's elbow. 'Have we got everything, my dear? Yes. Then come along. Just put it on the bill, Miss Meecham. Thank you. Good-day.' They went out.

Instinctively, with a quick silent interchange of glances, the three women yielded first place to the young man, who only wanted a stamp, was served and left. Whereupon, Miss Veevers turned to Miss Ward. 'Did you see that? The way he cut her short?'

'Almost pushed her out!'

'Because of young Gerald. You saw,' said Miss Cadwallader-Jones. 'Simply frightfully jealous of men with her.'

'She's very nice.'

'Very sensible. Got her feet on the ground – but him!'

'He's frightening. Good job he's retired, I wouldn't like to – '

'I think he's a little . . . You were there, that strange scene on the green last week, when the roundabout was there.'

'Oh, and the horse! *Wasn't* that queer?'

'What goes on in their cottage at night, I don't know. They've got very thick curtains but you can hear squeaking and bumping sounds from the upstairs room. Rhythmic.'

'Surely . . . ? *No!*'

'Sometimes, if you happen to be passing, you can catch faint flickers of shadow back and forth across the ceiling.'

'When they first moved in they had a simply huge crate with the furniture and I heard him call out to the moving men "Careful with Roddy!"'

'Who's that?'

'I'm sure I don't know. Oh yes, Miss Meecham, now what did I come for . . . ?'